# IF YOU THINK THIS IS *FIELD AND STREAM*, BOY, ARE YOU ALL WET!

With the help of a cranky ship, a lecherous bailiff, and a testy, telepathic dolphin from Earth, Judge Aleria Farrell must solve a perplexing puzzle. Some fishy victim is in great danger on the planet Kahiko—but which one?

The world's humanoid amphibians are eager to please—in more ways than one—and Aleria finds herself dazzled by their fantastic and amorous way of life amid fairyland coral cities. Electric eels supply heat, squid farms produce brilliant dyes, and luminescent fish provide lighting . . . and the Kahikans satisfy her every erotic whim. Aleria is hooked, and only her bailiff's magic can keep them from being the main course in a fish fry . . .

Other Pinnacle Books in
**These Lawless Worlds** series

#1: THE LOVE MACHINE

#2: SCALES OF JUSTICE

# THESE LAWLESS WORLDS

Jarrod Comstock

PINNACLE BOOKS  NEW YORK

> **ATTENTION: SCHOOLS AND CORPORATIONS**
>
> PINNACLE Books are available at quantity discounts with bulk purchases for educational, business or special promotional use. For further details, please write to: SPECIAL SALES MANAGER, Pinnacle Books, Inc., 1430 Broadway, New York, NY 10018.

This is a work of fiction. All the characters and events portrayed in this book are fictional, and any resemblance to real people or incidents is purely coincidental.

THESE LAWLESS WORLDS #2: SCALES OF JUSTICE

*Copyright © 1984 by Jarrod Comstock*

All rights reserved, including the right to reproduce this book or portions thereof in any form.

An original Pinnacle Books edition, published for the first time anywhere.

First printing/July 1984

ISBN: 0-523-42196-6

Can. ISBN: 0-523-43186-4

Cover art by Jerry Bingham

*Printed in the United States of America*

PINNACLE BOOKS, INC.
1430 Broadway
New York, New York 10018

9 8 7 6 5 4 3 2 1

# Acknowledgments

When one produces two books within five months of each other, many of the same people who contributed to the first continue to be involved in the production of the second. Ellen Kozak and Sharon Jarvis were there all along, of course. And Shulamith Saltzman's contribution to this series is an enduring one.

And *plus ça change, plus c'est la même chose*, so I must thank—again—Gert, Sid, and Warren Kozak, Ben Margolis, Karen Case, Diana and Marshall Segal, Carol Walkowiak, Dee McGarity, Alice Kehoe, Marzetta Doss, and my buddy, Steve McGarrett. To that list I must add June Kozak Kane and Hope Aldrich—and Joan Winston, for all that taping. Special thanks go to Gremlin, the dog who played cat, and to Carla Kozak, whose comment on Gremlin's actions inspired an important element of this book. Likewise, my appreciation to David Hartwell for introducing me to coprolites— everyone's education is lacking in some areas—and to Sarah Uman for her faith in this series.

I would be remiss, indeed, were I not to express my gratitude to Nada Vuckovic for her assistance and loyalty— and to thank Ginger, just because.

*Jarrod Comstock*
*January 1984*

No one but his lawyer and his agent has seen the reclusive JARROD COMSTOCK since he took to the hills to write this series. He lives alone on a wooded island, communicating with the outside world mostly by telephone and modem, closing in on his life's ambition—to become a hermit with a WATS line. Though his formal education ended years ago, he continues to be a perpetual student of the law, the sciences, history, philosophy, and languages. When you live alone on an island, he notes, you have a lot of time to devote to such things.

# Chapter 1

There was nothing new under the sun (an archaic phrase, stemming from a time when people were planetbound and thought the sun passed above them). And Levis Ostego, who drew his salary for a job that millions of others would have paid for the privilege of doing, was bored.

Levis sighed. The monitoring station should have been the most exciting place on Earth to work. Its huge receptors picked up every sort of message imaginable from the far reaches of space. Though most of those messages were merely relayed as addressed, those with incomplete forwarding information had to be translated and analyzed so that their proper addressees could be determined.

Since every impulse in every message passed through these monitors, working the station meant the opportunity—if one were so inclined—to eavesdrop. A curious monitor could be the first to know everything that was going on in the known universe—and a lot that happened beyond Confederation boundaries. Indeed, several wire services—archaic term, that; Levis wondered idly how it had originated—

offered a premium for reporting juicy bits of gossip to them.

Levis Ostego had never entertained thoughts of accepting the premium for wire service "stringing"—another archaic term whose origins eluded him. Doing so could have cost him his job. Dull as that job had turned out to be, it had certain social advantages.

It seemed to fascinate everyone who hadn't tried it. People he met, who at first tended to regard him as less than interesting, invariably began to pay rapt attention to him when they discovered what he did for a living. Convinced he was privy to the secrets of the universe and just playing it close to the vest, they hung around in droves, sometimes long enough to bother to get to know him. He had developed a number of relationships—especially with women, whom he normally found it difficult to get to know—in this way. Of course, they often lost interest when they found out how little he actually monitored. Still, it got his foot in the door (another expression whose origins eluded him).

Glancing over the monitors in his care, Levis harrumphed to himself; hadn't *he* once thought monitoring the most exciting job on Earth? Isn't that why he'd applied for it?

Actually, the job wasn't really *on* Earth. It was on a special space station that had orbited the home planet since ancient times. It had been rebuilt and updated, of course, but it still contained some antique segments from its original construction.

Now, *that* was something Levis, an amateur historian, found exciting. He spent much of his spare time poking around the outer ring and the inner core, trying to determine just how long a given module had been in place, and he was always thrilled when he found a piece of centuries-old aluminum or ceramic.

But message monitoring itself had proven incredibly dull. The electronic epistles—even those of the famous or infamous—took on a certain sameness after a month or two: "Darling, I've missed you. Wish you were here." "In response to your letter, please note that I've paid this bill, per receipt number . . . ." "When he told me he really didn't care whether or not I stayed, I got up and walked out. You should have seen his face!"

Levis's own freckled, open face no longer registered interest, even when those messages came from people the rest of the Confederation idolized. What was the old expression—"They put on their pants one leg at a time"? The famous, like everyone else, had ordinary problems with banks, neighbors, bill collectors, utility companies. If and when they did anything really exciting, they usually coded their messages.

Levis could have cracked the codes—he was a skilled cryptographer—but after the first few weeks, he had realized that what most people wanted to keep to themselves was best kept that way, if only because it was so dull. Now he seldom bothered cluttering his brain even with the contents of messages he scanned for the government's protection. Clever revolutionaries or criminals wouldn't use codes, anyway. They'd probably say things like "Meet me under the clock" for "Blow up the Capitol," and no one would ever guess their intentions.

Levis had come to think of himself as extraneous. Machines sorted the electronic mail, and the main part of his job was to make judgment calls on the messages the machines didn't know how to handle. These were rare, and usually required only an adjustment in a twenty-two-digit zip code. Now *there* was a term he really wondered about. What was zippy about a twenty-two-digit number? What had ever been?

Take that monitor in the corner, for example. It had just lit up and was ringing anxiously. Levis shrugged. Someone had probably sent a letter to Mozambique using the code for Manistique. It happened all the time.

Then Levis realized that the alarmist was a sublim, geared to pull telepathic messages out of deep space. The monitoring station had giant sublim dishes aimed in all directions, but they made few pickups. When they received something, they usually just recorded it for later analysis. They rarely sounded their alarms, for they seldom knew when to do so. A mechanical mind could pick up on a really powerful empathetic expression, but it took a living mind to comprehend and translate the untranslatable.

This machine, however, seemed to be trying to do a living mind's job. It was ringing for his assistance, but its screen was broadcasting a series of words—*words* on a sublim monitor! He watched with amazement as the screen formed the words *death* and *destruction*. The words faded, and the word *assist* appeared, then disappeared, melting into the original message.

Probably a joke set up by one of the other shift monitors, Levis thought, but best to verify it. He placed his hand on the sensor screen—and the emotional impact sent him crashing backward against the rail that defined the edge of the walkway between the machines. Here indeed was a message of death and destruction, an image of terror so strong that even a machine could read its meaning. But though the subject was clear enough, its details weren't. *Where* was it coming from? And was *it* being destroyed—or was it *threatening* destruction? Levis adjusted the dials, but the message refused to clarify itself.

There was only one course of action open to him, Levis decided. He'd have to take this to Medina; it was more along the lines of her specialty. He made up a duplicate disc. When he picked it up, he discovered that, even when recorded on inert material and wrapped in a protective envelope, the message seemed to tingle through his fingers, up his arm: *death, destruction*.

Levis was seized by a feeling of urgency. Setting the machines on automatic alarm mode—except for the sublim monitor, which had done quite enough alarming—he took off down the corridor toward his supervisor's office. Perhaps Medina could figure out what it meant. If not, they'd have to call for outside assistance.

One thing was certain, though. Levis wasn't bored anymore.


"There's a regular pattern to it, but there's something fishy about the way it's coming through." Medina Meltor spread her graphs out on her supervisor's desk. "See, here"—she pointed to one of them—"and *here*."

"Fishy?" Jedrek Kabeel bellowed. Medina and her assistant, Levis Ostego, jumped back a pace. "*Fishy*? Do you mean someone's been playing games with our monitoring equipment?"

"Oh, no, that isn't what I meant at all—"

"Well, then, say what you mean!" Kabeel ordered.

"I did, sir," Medina told him, as calmly as he could. "I get a distinct impression of water, of—well, fish."

"Broadcasting telepathically over the interstellar void? *Fish*? Impossible!"

"Mr. Kabeel, sir, there *are* instances. Dolphin Rings, for example—"

"Dolphin Rings can't send telepathy through the interstellar void," Kabeel growled. He was a large man, and his position of authority made him seem even larger, an impression that was aggravated by his tendency to raise his voice.

"Or won't," Medina suggested cautiously; you didn't correct Jedrek Kabeel. "We've never verified the outside limits of their range. They won't let us."

"Damned fish."

"They're mammals, sir," Levis ventured.

"Arrogant *fish*!" Kabeel boomed, and both Medina and Levis jumped back two paces. Both of them were well aware of their irascible chief's low boiling point and knew enough not to get him riled up about a minor matter. But this message hadn't felt like a minor matter to Medina.

She was a psychotech, class I, and she knew a telepathic message when she felt one. She also knew that telepathic messages traveled across the galaxies far faster than the speed of light. They accounted for a phenomenon that people used to blame on phases of the moon or changes in barometric pressure—those strange moods that often seemed to affect whole populations suddenly and without apparent cause. Even if this message weren't urgent, it was undoubtedly contemporaneous.

But it did feel urgent to Medina, and also frightening enough to warrant incurring Kabeel's wrath.

"Sir," she ventured, "I really do think we ought to summon a Dolphin Ring. I can't interpret the message myself—it's beyond my abilities—but I'm sure it's a message of danger. Whether it's danger to us or to someone else, that *is* what we're supposed to be on the lookout for. The Confederation contract—"

"*I* know our duties under our Confederation contract," Kabeel growled. "I also know that if we cause this much of a stir, if we call in those damned fish—"

"Mammals," Levis muttered softly.

"Fish!" Kabeel stated flatly. "If we call them in, and pay them, and if you're wrong about this signal, heads are going to roll here, and they're not going to be mine!"

Levis gulped, but Medina stood her ground. She understood the corporate mentality of IC&C—Interstellar Communications and Corroborations—as well as anyone. If you cost the company money, it cost you your job. But she also knew what she'd felt from that transmission. There had been just one single burst of thought—they'd been unable to find a record of any previous transmission or any repetition—but that single flash had struck terror into Medina, into Levis, and even into that poor subliminal monitor. If it could terrify a machine, she ought to report it to the government, even if doing so put her job on the line.

Medina was confident that the findings of the Dolphin Ring would justify having called it in, and said as much.

"You really think so?" Kabeel asked dubiously. His change of mood was marked. It was rare that any of his subordinates stood up to him, rarer still that he couldn't browbeat them into backing down. When he ran into an underling who couldn't be swayed, Kabeel tended to listen.

"I do," Medina affirmed.

"All right," sighed the rotund crew chief. "Bring in the damned fish."

"Better not let them hear you call them that," Levis cautioned.

"I won't say a word."

Medina couldn't resist taking one more jab at her arrogant boss. "Don't forget that they're telepaths," she warned him, in the cheeriest tone she could muster.

"I won't," Kabeel said glumly. But his face reflected his dismay at the implications of her warning. As they left, Medina and Levis heard him muttering to himself, "Mammals, mammals, mammals."

The mammals in question were less than pleased to interrupt their contemplation of the meaning of life in order to convene a Ring. They devoted their lives to the study of philosophy, a study that was eternal, since it asked many questions but seldom, if ever, answered even one. When not philosophizing, dolphins invariably devoted their time to the physical workouts that human beings often mistook for play. *Mens sana in corpore sano* had always been the golden rule by which the dolphin community lived.

They also had an abiding urge to help the needy. Their race had always felt compelled to do so. This compulsion was responsible for the legends of dolphins that had saved drowning innocents in ancient times and the stories of schools of dolphins that had borne dying pilot whales to the surface so they could breathe their last.

Playing on their sympathy, the Confederation had persuaded four dolphins to interrupt their philosophizing to form a Ring Minor. It took twelve to form a Ring Major, and there didn't seem to be time enough to convene that many dolphins from the far waters of the earth and ship them to the monitoring station. The dolphins didn't give a hoot about danger to human civilization. Their race had seen the great hairless apes rise, fall, and rise again, and while they might watch out for the safety of individual men, danger to man's life-style and works was not their concern.

Playing down the hint of threat in the untranslatable message, the Confederation had appealed to the dolphins on the premise that this could have been a Mayday call (another of those terms whose origins Levis Ostego wondered about).

Now Levis wondered whether that argument might not influence the dolphins' interpretation of the message. He said as much to Medina, who dismissed his fears on that score.

"Dolphins are philosophers," she told him. "To them, nothing can be stated in absolutes. If they aren't completely certain of what the message says, they'll give us a lot of double-talk. Then we can either send them home or convene a Ring Major."

"Or hope for another message from our unknown telepaths," Levis appended.

Medina nodded. The two of them were waiting in the cargo bay airlock for the bay pressure to be brought to the proper level for the unloading of the dolphins, who would then be wrapped in wet spongecloth and rushed to a specially salinated fish tank in the outermost ring. Gravity hovered close to one G in the outer ring of the monitoring station. The dolphins preferred it a little bit higher, but they could make do with that.

There were four of them, all bottle-nosed, all male. According to the shuttle's manifest, their names were Carswell, Rosmer, Selmar, and Sebrook.

Levis had never worked with dolphins. In fact, his only prior encounter with members of the species had been a memorable grammar school field trip; he'd been briefly introduced to two who were in the entertainment business at a sea park. They had fascinated him then, just as Carswell, Rosmer, Selmar, and Sebrook fascinated him now. He couldn't wait to meet them.

But the dolphins, it seemed, were far less eager to meet *him*, or any of the other monitoring-station staff. The moment they were unloaded from the shuttle, they began to communicate their unhappiness at being off-planet in no uncertain terms. That those complaints were conveyed telepathically made them impossible to ignore—a kind of intrusion that Levis understood to be considered very bad manners among telepaths.

Levis tried to prevent the dolphins' vibes—another curious archaic term—from making him testy; he had a fairly high empathetic quotient himself. *They're just suffering from space lag*, he told himself. *They'll be okay once they adjust*. But the thought came, unbidden, that if the message were really as urgent as it seemed, there wouldn't be time for the dolphins to adjust.

He resigned himself to dealing with their ill humor. *I guess we're stuck with them*, he thought.

*We're stuck with you, too.* The thought blasted through his brain with all the combined power of the Dolphin Ring.

"Hey!" Levis protested aloud.

Medina, who had obviously felt the same telepathic blast—it must have been broadcast rather than directed—voiced a more coherent retort. "You aren't here to read our thoughts; you're here to read a message and help pinpoint its source. Nasty comments like that betray your bad manners in reading us and in communicating back so clearly!"

The dolphins were instantly contrite. *Sorry*, they

narrowcast back, just to Levis and Medina. *We are, quite literally, out of our element.*

*You might say "littorally,"* the one named Rosmer interjected. The others—and the two humans—groaned.

*The young man was right*, Selmar, who seemed to be in charge of the Ring, continued. *We suffer from space lag. Dolphins are very susceptible to that ailment.*

"Don't let it worry you," Medina consoled them. "I've had it a few times myself. I understand."

*Thank you*, came the wave of thought from all four of the creatures Kabeel had referred to as fish. Levis couldn't help thinking, as they moved along the corridor, that if these were fish, they qualified very well for the old expression "fish out of water."

*So we are*, the dolphin named Carswell chuckled, *about as far out of our home waters as we can get!*

"Well, we can remedy that somewhat," Levis told them. They had arrived at the specially salinated tank. "Your quarters may be a bit small, but we hope you'll find them comfortable."

The sigh of mingled pleasure and relief that emanated from all four guests as they entered the tank told Levis that they were indeed satisfied with their accommodations.

"We'll give you a few moments to yourselves to get oriented," Medina told them. "Then we'd like to get right to work on the subject."

*Right*, bubbled Selmar. *We'll be ready fairly soon.*

"Good." Medina nodded. "Levis and I will get our equipment. We'll be right back."

*Not* that *soon!* the dolphins protested. But Medina merely smiled and dragged Levis off to fetch the message discs and all the data the monitors had thus far collected regarding them. Speed in interpretation was an absolute necessity.

Even if the dolphins could figure out what the message really meant and who had sent it, that would only start it through channels.

Levis realized that Medina was trying to make up, on their end, for the delays that would undoubtedly occur when the message was forwarded to Confederation headquarters. It was hopeless, rather like speeding to a destination when you were already late. You couldn't possibly arrive on time; you could only be a little less late. By the time the Confederation bureaucrats got around to making a decision, the distant telepaths who had sent the message would either be dead or—if they intended to attack—would be *here*.

Still, Levis had sensed the desperate urgency of that message. Remembering how that had felt, he quickened his pace as he and Medina hurried along the great curving corridors to retrieve the materials the Dolphin Ring would need.

# Chapter II

*What's so urgent that you had to interrupt my leave?* Judge Aleria Farrell of the Fourteenth Judicial Circuit of the Confederation of Planets thought darkly. The transponder implant at the base of her skull reverberated with her annoyance at having this, her first vacation in years, interrupted, and she knew Houston could feel the angry vibrations on his end of the link.

Aleria was always annoyed when Houston used the privacy override to intrude on her thoughts. He didn't do it often, but every time was once too often in Aleria's opinion. Although technically she controlled the activation of the implant by removing her special control ring from her left hand, Houston had the power to contact her telepathically if an emergency arose.

The problem was that the ship tended to be an alarmist. It was a mistake to give a machine—even a sentient machine like Houston—that much discretion, the judge mused. But after thinking about it for a moment, Aleria decided that she would rather have him—she always thought of

Houston as somewhat male, as did he, she guessed—she would rather have him interrupt her too often than ignore something that did, in fact, require her immediate attention.

*You took long enough to come to that conclusion*, Houston remarked smugly.

Aleria, who had momentarily forgotten the link was still on, silently screamed back at him that he had invaded her privacy and she would trade him in for the malfunctioning monster he was. *They'll bust you down to garbage scow*, she threatened, pleased at the thought.

Houston was *not* pleased at the image, and Aleria, who realized that she had been doing the telepathic equivalent of shouting, sensed the ship madly scrambling to moderate the volume at his end of the link.

*I warned you not to take your leave on Earth*, Houston commented dolefully. *You know this always happens when we're accessible.*

*What happens*? Aleria snapped, but in her heart she already knew.

Houston confirmed her worst fears. *Judge Ashippun wants you to report to Judicial Central as soon as you can get there—no later than five o'clock this afternoon.*

Aleria cursed under her breath. "I wanted a chance to show Jemall the beauties of my home planet," she said out loud. The big alien bailiff, basking in the warm sunlight on the golden sand beach, looked up lazily when he heard her mention his name. Obviously, Houston hadn't activated Jemall's transponder, and the silver-scaled Acetan was blissfully unaware of the conversation that had just taken place.

"Problem?" he asked.

"Houston just contacted me. The vacation's over."

"So soon? What's up?"

Glancing at her companion's naked body, Aleria fought of the impulse to reply, "You appear to be." Instead, she told him seriously, "Ashippun wants to see us in his chambers, pronto."

Jemall raised his eyebrows—or what would have been his eyebrows, had he been human; on the hairless Acetan, they were merely pronounced ridges on his forehead. "You know," he remarked thoughtfully, "if it's this urgent, it might be a pretty important case."

*Or a reprimand*, Houston suggested worriedly. He had extended the link to include the bailiff.

"Just what I need, a paranoid ship," Aleria muttered.

*Well, it could happen.*

"Look, Houston." Aleria spelled it out slowly and carefully. "I know the law. I know the limits of my authority. And I do my best. As long as that's true, the worst they can do is reverse a decision on appeal. So I'm not worried about any reprimands, and I'll thank you to keep your paranoia to yourself." *It can be catching*, she added silently.

The ship flashed her a mental apology. He was nothing if not loyal, and he knew that Aleria didn't find it easy being the Confederation's sole judicial standard-bearer in that far quadrant of the galaxy that constituted her circuit. The Confederation was a loose alliance, and its central government had no real authority over the laws of its various worlds, except where they came into conflict with one another—or when an off-planet judge was summoned to rule on a matter deemed too sensitive for the local judiciary. When that happened, Aleria, like all the other circuit judges, often made up the rules—based on sound equitable principles, of course—as she went along.

That, inevitably, brought complaints. But no one since

the beginning of time had ever left a courtroom totally satisfied with any judge's verdict. The Confederation's Judicial Conference understood this, and most complaints died aborning. But there was always the possibility that one—

Aleria put the thought out of her mind and flashed a wordless reprimand at Houston for having placed the seed of it there.

"Maybe it *is* an interesting case," she mused aloud. "I guess I could use a little mental exercise."

"A little *physical* exercise wouldn't hurt, either," Jemall noted, slapping her gently on her shapely bottom.

Aleria stuck out her tongue at him. "Are you implying that I'm fat?" she demanded, knowing full well that she wasn't. The judge was just a little bit vain about the prime condition in which she kept her body, which was tall—nearly two meters tall—and lean as a dancer's.

*An ounce of prevention is worth pounds of diet*, Houston chimed in piously.

"Are you still listening?" Aleria was indignant.

*You didn't tell me not to.*

"Well, scram. Leave us alone. Let us enjoy the last few moments of this vacation without being monitored."

*To hear is to obey*, the ship responded mockingly.

But before he could break the link, Aleria stopped him momentarily. "Did Judge Ashippun give you any reason at all for wanting to see us?"

*No. He just chuckled and said he hoped you liked water.*

"See? I told you it wasn't a reprimand! He wouldn't have laughed if we were in trouble," Aleria told the ship.

"We *are* in trouble," Jemall countered. "*I* don't like water—not one bit!"

"I know, baby," Aleria said, reaching out to console

him. He reached for her, and his long, four-jointed fingers began to play gently along her bare, sun-warmed sides. Aleria shivered at the electric sensation and moved closer to him.

*Disgusting*, the ship muttered, and broke the link, leaving the flame-haired judge and her silver-scaled bailiff alone to arouse each other as they lay entwined on the golden sand.

Getting the sand out of her hair had been a problem, and Aleria was still brushing her long red tresses as Jemall pulled their hovercraft up to the imposing entrance of Judicial Central. The judge set down her brush and deftly coiled the coppery tangle around her her head in a style that befit the dignity of her position. Checking her appearance in the aircar's rearview reflector, she pronounced it acceptable, and sprang out onto the docking ramp. She smoothed the layered panels of her ankle-length skirt into place as she waited for Jemall to relinquish the controls of the craft to the parking attendant and join her at the security check.

Aleria noticed that Jemall was responding to this, his first visit to Judicial Central, with atypical propriety. He had abandoned the garish color combinations he usually wore for the latest in Earth fashions—a flowing white shirt belted into voluminous black silk pants. The pants were tucked into—and ballooned over—calf-high black kid boots. Jemall's addiction to bright hues was evident only in the brilliant and elaborate embroidery that covered the shirt's collar and full sleeves.

His only other adornment was what appeared to be an oblong enameled brooch at his waist. Actually, it was the hilt of his knife, a superdense object that he had condensed from the molecules of the scimitar he usually carried, by means of the psionic matter transmutation that was the special talent of Acetans. Jemall, like other natives of his planet, wore clothing only for its decorative effect, but felt totally naked when he wasn't sporting a weapon. And, despite its weight, he preferred one with enough substance so that he could transmute it into something with a heft to it if the need arose.

Aleria wore no weapons here on the home planet, but she felt strangely naked without her laser pistol. She had worn it strapped to her thigh since that long-ago day when she had left the more civilized planets to serve as an appointed defender. But carrying concealed weapons was banned here on Earth, except by those, like Jemall, whose jobs required them.

Aleria was also clad in the latest Earth fashion. The panels of her multilayered white gown curved at the hem like the petals of a flower. The tops of the panels were woven into a twisted cord that fastened behind her neck, halter fashion, leaving the tawny skin of her arms, shoulders, and most of her back bare.

Aleria and Jemall paused for a moment to watch as their hovercraft, under the guidance of its parking drone, swooped among the high towers to the holding area, where it would remain until they summoned it. When it had disappeared into the clouds—a clever solution to the parking problem, Aleria reflected—the judge and her bailiff proceeded through the security check at Judicial Central's entrance.

Identification was by retinal scan. The automatic scanner confirmed Aleria's identification and verified that she was expected. But the weapons sensor went crazy when Jemall tried to follow her. It threw up an automatic force barrier around the bailiff while it tried to scan his eyes—

which, being Acetan, did not contain typical human rod-and-cone cell patterning.

From outside the force barrier, where Aleria stood watching, the big silver Acetan seemed to be encased in a rainbow of dancing color, which reflected off the fine scales of his body. It took what seemed to be a very long time before the scanner was able to identify Jemall to its satisfaction and verify his right to enter the building while carrying a weapon. Confirmation of his job status did this. Jemall was not only cleared; he was *required* to wear his weapon at all times, even—no, especially—here in Judicial Central. A bailiff was, after all, charged with enforcing order in the courtroom and protecting the judge to whose court he was attached.

Bearing arms was a privilege that Aleria, for all of her judicial authority, did not share. The rules of the home planet left her totally dependent on the protection provided by her bailiff—except for the miniature explosive charge contained in her transponder-activating ring. And even though Judicial Central was as safe an environment as she would ever encounter, even though she had total trust in Jemall's loyalty and his protective impulses, Aleria still did not enjoy the sensation of loss of control that haunted her whenever she could not feel her weapon in its accustomed position against her thigh. She had long ago ceased to be aware of its presence, but found herself conscious of its absence with every step as she crossed the lobby.

An elevator whisked them toward the twenty-ninth floor, and Aleria seized on those few seconds to shrug off her unease and force composure on herself. Maybe it was the lack of her accustomed weapon, but she found she needed to convince herself that she now really *was* a judge and that Seifi Ashippun, whose summons she was answering, was her friend as well as her mentor.

Judicial Central had always had this effect on her. Even though the sensation was a fleeting one, she always caught herself feeling like the accused when she entered the building. When that passed, she felt, once again, like the fledgling appointed counsel she had once been, in this same courthouse, years ago—always on her way to argue a hopeless case.

"Funny how some environments affect you psychologically," Aleria commented to Jemall. The bailiff, who had never seen her exhibit the slightest hesitancy before, looked bewildered.

"Well, maybe this place wouldn't get to *you*," the judge continued, "since you're from Aceta, but to me, Judicial Central is a symbol. I was raised in awe of what it stands for. It's difficult for me to believe I'm really a judge now, that I actually belong here."

"You don't," Jemall replied bluntly.

"What the hell do you mean by that?"

"You don't belong in a stuffy building like this," he explained. "You belong on Houston, out in the distant reaches of the galaxy. So do I. This place gives me the creeps."

Aleria looked at him in alarm. When Jemall got the creeps, he did so literally. Acetans, who molted regularly anyway, tended to shed their skins under conditions of stress. When Jemall said that something made his skin crawl, he often meant it. Aleria had never grown used to seeing his almost transparent discarded skins around the ship, and she didn't fancy having him leave a trail of them in the corridors of Judicial Central. But she noted with relief that he seemed to be speaking figuratively, at least for now.

Jemall, of course, had not been raised in a tradition that caused him to hold this building in awe. In fact, having never been to earth before, his only contacts with the judicial headquarters had occurred when he had applied for his position—and whenever he had to file a request or a report for Aleria. That had happened just enough times for him to develop a hearty dislike and a healthy disregard for the bureaucratic side of his job which, for Jemall, was all Judicial Central represented.

He had qualified for his position and been sworn in as bailiff without ever leaving deep space, having done so at the same time that Aleria had been appointed to the bench. She had been promoted from appointed defender when Judge Ashippun was summoned home to join the Court of Appeals. Aleria had always wondered just how much of her current status she owed to Judge Ashippun's hearty recommendations and how much to the fortunate circumstance of being the only qualified attorney readily available out there in the Fourteenth Circuit.

Aleria knew what Jemall's impression of Judicial Central was. He saw it as the source of an annoying abundance of paperwork. That was a curious term, she reflected; like its synonym, *red tape*, it expressed an ancient concept whose real meaning was lost in history. Both terms now meant the same thing—the endless computerized information that was required by law but served no apparent purpose, since most of it just disappeared into the databanks and was never seen again. But if Jemall failed to be impressed by Judicial Central, it remained, for Aleria, the focal point of all of her aspirations, as it had been since her childhood. She was just a little bit envious of his attitude, but could never have been so nonchalant about this courthouse, though the courtrooms of other planets did not impress her. In fact, she and Jemall had developed a favorite way of breaking in the courtrooms to which she was assigned, one that gave them both a certain amount of physical exercise and a delicious sense of having got away with something.

But here—well, maybe it was just a consequence of Houston's alarmism or her own weaponless state. Even though she was now a judge, Aleria still felt just a little insecure.

The elevator spat them out on the twenty-ninth floor, and the judge and her bailiff found themselves in a foyer with two doors, one of which read "Court of Appeals, Branch II, Seifi Ashippun Presiding." The other door led to Branch I, where Meenon Suamico sat.

Aleria took a deep breath, drew herself up to her full imposing height, and opened the door. She swept in as regally as she could, with Jemall following at her heels, only to discover that she needn't have worried. Judge Ashippun's reception was instantaneous and enthusiastic.

The white-haired judge, who fit no description so much as that of a merry old man, had been dictating an order to his robotic clerk. When he saw Aleria, he shut off the input mike and bounced across his mahogany-paneled courtroom—which would have been quite austere but for his jovial presence—to plant an affectionate kiss on her cheek.

"Welcome, welcome, my dear," he bubbled. "Come in, come in. You, too, Jemall. Come on back to my private digs and have a cup of tea, a drink, whatever you want. It's good to see you again, both of you."

Aleria felt all the tension leave her body. Old Ashippun, with his merry eyes, and button nose, reminded her of one of Santa's elves. He appeared to be delighted with himself, his work, his guests. He kept up a happy patter as he ushered Aleria and Jemall through his chambers and into his private quarters.

"This building was designed for workaholics. You see, I'm never far from my office, and my bailiff has a small apartment on the other side of the chambers. Our balconies adjoin. Judge Suamico's bailiff's balcony adjoins my bailiff's, and his own is just beyond. Each side of the building is the same—two courts and one elevator."

Judge Ashippun led Aleria and Jemall through his living room onto what he called his balcony, actually a broad terrace overlooking the building's central courtyard. Far below, Aleria could see the pool and tennis court; Judicial Central was not without its amenities.

"We have a rule here," Judge Ashippun confided, "that there can be no crosstalk from balcony to balcony. In the early years, when the building was first occupied, the judges used to call to each other across the courtyard. It's a real temptation even now. But the apartments reverberated with the din, and, of course, it meant an absolute end to confidentiality. We had to put a stop to it." He grinned sheepishly. "I say 'we,' but of course I wasn't here then. It's amazing how quickly one takes on the native coloration, my dear."

Aleria smiled. "I see your terrace has taken on considerable non-native coloration."

Indeed, it was covered with an incredible variety of plants, most of which Judge Ashippun had picked up in his space travels. A great number of them were sealed under glass domes to provide them with appropriate artificial environments, but nearly as many others bloomed in pots and jars, or climbed the trellises that marked the edges of the terrace, and ran across the overhang formed by the balcony above.

The broad terrace was a riot of color and scent, which carried over into Judge Ashippun's living room. There, more plants hung from the ceiling in decorative baskets and stood on every available surface in ceramic pots of assorted sizes and hues. Aleria smiled again, remembering Houston's relief when Judge Ashippun had finally sent these plants back to earth. Their presence had always been a sore point with the ship who, though he adored Judge Ashippun, had complained often and vociferously about having a jungle in his belly. In fact, Houston had agreed to ferry Aleria around only on the condition that she bring no plants aboard.

Aleria got around this by bringing on an occasional bunch of cut flowers, but in her tenure the bulkheads had not bloomed, and Houston was grateful. He had even said so, several times.

A robot server appeared with a tray of ornate pastries; gourmet cooking was another of Judge Ashippun's hobbies. As Aleria and Jemall settled back into the plush lounge chairs to enjoy the refreshments, Aleria remarked casually that she hadn't realized this was to be a social visit.

"Houston made it sound imperative—"

"It was," Judge Ashippun replied.

"He also implied that it was serious."

"It is. We need you to take on a fact-finding hearing immediately."

"Here on Earth?" Jemall interrupted, between mouthfuls.

"I'm afraid not." Judge Ashippun shook his head.

"Nearby?" the bailiff asked hopefully.

Judge Ashippun squelched that hope. "It's about as far away as you can get and still be in this galaxy."

"Terrific," Aleria said sarcastically. "I really need a good case of space lag. I *am* supposed to be on leave, you know."

"I know," the other judge replied.

"Couldn't you send someone else?"

"Actually, we can't. We've had an appeal from a race that claims it's being annihilated. The transmission was short and somewhat garbled. We had to convene a Ring Minor to interpret it."

"So *that's* what you meant about liking water," Jemall said with relief. "Well, I guess I can handle the company of a tuna or two."

"You're going to have the company of a dolphin, but only one. We'll have enough trouble shipping even that one under the necessary pressure and moisture conditions."

Aleria looked up. "How—?" she began.

"Houston is being fitted with a tank, of course. It'll just about fill your main cabin. Things will be fairly cramped for you, but there's a warp route; the trip won't take you more than two weeks."

Aleria saw her chance for physical fun and games with Jemall—which was how they usually passed their time in the interstellar void—vanish out the porthole if all the space in the main cabin was to be taken up by a tank. Jemall's wry face reflected his disappointment at that prospect.

"Why me?" Aleria demanded.

Judge Ashippun shrugged. "You're a judge, and you're a sensitive. We can ship only one dolphin, but he may need the assistance of a Ring. As a sensitive, you should be able to reinforce him to a degree."

"I've never tried it. The theory could be all wet," Aleria replied.

But the usually merry Judge Ashippun didn't even crack a smile. "You'll have to do your best. It's a water world. I've heard that water is a better conductor of telepathic impulses than the nitrogen-oxygen mixture of our atmosphere." He looked over at Jemall, who seemed suddenly to have lost the sheen from his scales. "Is something wrong?"

Jemall hesitated.

"Acetans don't like water," Aleria explained.

"Well, if you'd rather take another bailiff—"

"No!" Aleria and Jemall cried in unison.

"So *that's* how it is with you two," Judge Ashippun chuckled. "I suspected as much."

Aleria looked at him innocently. "I'm sure I don't know what you're talking about," she said, smiling sweetly. "Besides, Jemall won't have any trouble on a water planet."

"I won't?" the bailiff asked dubiously.

Aleria nodded. "You can use psionic matter transmutation on yourself," she told him.

"And do what?"

"I don't know. What's amphibious?" She paused; a devilish gleam crept into her eye. "Got it!" she cried.

"Got what?"

"You can *frog* yourself."

This time Judge Ashippun laughed so hard he upset his coffee onto the plush white carpeting.

Jemall, however, merely smiled smugly. "You're gonna have to kiss this toad a lot before he turns back into a handsome prince."

Aleria blushed to the roots of her flame-colored hair, and Judge Ashippun glanced from her to the bailiff and back again with the triumphant look of one who had uncovered a secret he had been sure of, all along.

# Chapter III

*You're being too secretive*, Rosmer complained.

Aleria reflected that the bottle-nosed dolphin seemed to complain about almost everything. She attributed it to his having been confined for so long in the small pressurized tank, which allowed him barely enough room to turn around, let alone frolic as dolphins were inclined to do.

Aleria herself was none too comfortable. She had wedged herself into the minuscule space between the tank wall and Houston's bulkhead in order to get as close to the dolphin as she could without actually getting into the tank. She was trying to learn to set her telepathic vibrations on the same frequency as his. The idea was to enhance their individual capacities by uniting them, but their success—if you could call it that—had been very limited.

*You've got to open your mind to me fully before I can teach you how to screen your private thoughts. You're holding back. You've got to try to trust me.*

"I am trying," Aleria retorted. "There must be some other barrier. Maybe the glass of the tank?"

*It isn't the glass; it's you.*

Aleria knew he was right; she *was* resisting a full merger. She didn't really want Rosmer to read her mind and then play back its contents for the amusement of the other Orono when he returned home.

*I'd never do that*, Rosmer assured her. *It wouldn't be ethical. Besides, the Orono are not amused by the contents of human minds; we find them untidy and extremely unaesthetic.*

"Thanks a lot," Aleria hissed at him. "Just what I've always wanted—to have a damned fish tell me I've got an ugly mind."

*I will try to ignore your derogatory remark since I know that you know I'm not a fish. And you know full well that I never said you had an ugly mind. Please do not put words into my mouth that are not there.*

"They may not have been in your mouth, but I've seen them in your mind," Aleria told him.

*When did I say your mind was ugly?*

"You just did. Just now."

*You've forgotten your first lesson in mind-merging: Do not expand on or extrapolate from another's thoughts. To do so violates the code of honor by which my people live: "Tell only what you actually know. If reporting what someone else knows, making sure to capture every phrase. Never inject your own interpretations." Now, shall we try it again?*

Aleria set her jaw stubbornly. She did not like Rosmer's superior tone. And she liked the idea of relinquishing control over the contents of her mind even less.

*I know that*, said the dolphin. *But that's precisely why we have to practice the techniques of opening and closing the mind here and now. The Orono keep their code of ethics. I can be trusted. But we don't know anything about the ethics of those genocidal maniacs who live where we're headed.*

Aleria knew he was right, and apologized for putting a roadblock in the way of his training efforts. "I guess we're all out of sorts because of the crowding," she told him. "I'll be glad when this trip is over." Ten days of having to share their quarters with his tank had Aleria putting up mental walls, Jemall sulking in the cargo bay airlock, and Houston complaining constantly, in a low but audible buzz, about having to revolve while he warped through space. His spinning created the centrifugal force that kept the air and water in the dolphin's tank separate.

Aleria and Jemall were less than comfortable with this attempt on Houston's part at creating artificial gravity. His diameter was small, and his constant revolutions had a tendency to make them feel queasy. Aleria hadn't been space-sick in years, and she didn't enjoy the sensation.

Since the spinning was necessary in order to keep their passenger alive, Aleria, Houston, and Jemall tolerated it—though just barely. All three were counting the moments till planetfall.

Which would be in less than four days, Aleria reminded herself. She had better learn how to augment Rosmer and do it fast. "Maybe if I got into the tank?" she suggested.

"No!" Houston and Rosmer screamed, one aloud and the other mentally, but nevertheless in unison and in the same tone of alarm.

*There's not enough room*, was the dolphin's excuse.

"I'm not maintaining a high enough G-force," the ship explained. "The water will diffuse."

"All right," Aleria conceded. "I guess that wasn't the greatest idea." She sighed and resigned herself to tackling her training exercises once more. "Let's try it again." She rested her forehead against the cool glass wall of the tank and concentrated on matching her mind's limited telepathic channels to the dolphin's.

And then it happened. There was a merging, a matching, a linking. Suddenly her mind was one with the dolphin's. And she knew what it was like to cut through the sparkling waves of the ocean on a sunny day, knew all the discomfort of the tank, knew the taste of kelp, the meaning of the cries of gulls and of the keening of the humpback whales. One with Rosmer, she felt, as he did, the memory of cool water rushing against the sleek smoothness of his sides, knew the taste of the salt sea, even shared with him other, more personal memories: friends, family, joys, pain—even the pleasurable urgency of an erection, and the ecstasy he knew in relieving it.

*Sorry*, she told him, when she realized how she had invaded his privacy. Then it occurred to her that he had had equal access to *her* mind. Still linked with him, she knew that, having read *her* memories and the images carried there, the dolphin would have blushed if he had been able to do so.

Aleria shrugged at his embarrassment. Jemall could be very inventive at times, and she herself was no slouch when it came to devising new variations on what the law generally referred to as "deviant acts between consenting adults." She was never sure exactly what these acts ostensibly deviated from; as far as she could gather from her travels and her readings, there were no norms.

*Sorry*, she told the dolphin again. This time she was apologizing for what he'd shown instead of what she'd seen. *I thought you were going to protect my privacy*, she added. *You didn't even protect your own.*

*But I did! Your secrets are safe with me. And, to ensure that they'll be safe from others, too, let me teach you how to screen and block. After that, I'll teach you to augment. You have the gift, my dear. You'll have no difficulty in a Ring Minor, once you're trained properly.*

*You're sure of that?*

*I am.*

*But can I learn in four days?* Aleria asked.

*You can learn enough to get by. You'll be just fine.*

*What about what you've learned about me?* Aleria demanded once again.

*Never fear, fair damsel. Your dread secrets are safe with me. Now let's get back to business*, he ordered.

*Yes, let's*, Aleria replied, and determinedly set her mind to the task at hand.

The reward for her effort came only two days later, when the ship snapped out of warp, for the telepathic garbage of the interstellar void, which had been muted in hyperspace, reverberated in her brain whenever she tried to form an augmentation link with Rosmer—and sometimes even when she didn't. She had obviously begun to develop her own telepathic capability, and she was grateful that he'd helped her—no, forced her—to learn to screen. The technique worked on any transmissions, warding off the bombardment from the outside even as it shielded the thoughts that she wanted to keep to herself.

Aleria and the dolphin put their heads together, with the glass wall of the tank between them, and sorted through this telepathic flotsam and jetsam, trying to pinpoint any emission that might have originated at their destination. There were, it turned out, a considerable number. None repeated the cry for help that had summoned them here, but a great many seemed to be planetwide transmissions—news broadcasts, dramas, and the like.

Natives of the planet—who called themselves Kahikans, and their planet Kahiko—apparently used telepathy the way members of science-oriented civilizations used radio, television, telephones, and the mails. As Aleria and Rosmer eavesdropped on more of their transmissions, the reason became apparent; Kahiko was completely covered by water. It had no significant land masses, just a few rocks and coral reefs and a single small island called Rix, which the natives apparently revered as the fount of life and knowledge.

Houston cast a telescopic eye at their destination and was able to verify the total absence of land masses.

"That explains why they have no technology," Aleria noted dryly. "You don't develop machinery, internal combustion engines, or even fire, in a world where everything is submerged."

*A society doesn't need machinery, internal combustion engines, or even fire,* Rosmer reminded her. *We Orono have done quite well without them.*

"Oh, yeah?" snorted Houston. "You wouldn't be out here if it weren't for a machine—me!"

*I would be content to spend my days in my home waters. I did not need to spin through space in this tank.*

"Then why *are* you here?" the ship wanted to know.

*This is a mission of mercy,* the dolphin replied loftily.

But Aleria, monitoring the telepathic equivalent of a daytime soap opera, was not so sure. "I hope we haven't come all this way on a wild goose chase," she worried.

"In this instance, it would be a wild *fish* chase," Jemall pointed out. "What makes you think it might be a false alarm?"

"These dramas. They radiate from the Kahikan atmosphere and must permeate it. They're organized so that they don't overlap one another, and I think they must represent some sort of entertainment network, though they don't require actors, just storytellers. They broadcast whatever they see in their mind's eye—and you see it, too."

*That's how all the denizens of Earth's seas retell their legends,* Rosmer shrugged.

"But it's just like being there," Aleria marveled.

Rosmer wasn't impressed. *There's nothing new under the waves,* he noted. *That's an old Orono saying. But let me tell you, Aleria, that transmission we received was no drama. It was too strong. The whole ring felt it. It was a cry for help. But who could have sent it? And why?*

Houston had been keeping his telescope trained on Kahiko. He seized on Rosmer's questions to report his spectroanalysis of the planet.

"It seems to be teeming with life," he announced. "The atmosphere is quite humid. There seems to be evaporation and condensation going on constantly. Temperatures vary much as Earth's do from pole to equator, and the salt content of the Kahikan ocean seems to range from twenty-five to thirty parts per thousand."

Rosmer suddenly became very agitated. *That's too low,* he protested.

"What do you mean?" Aleria asked.

*Earth's oceans are normally thirty-three to thirty-eight parts per thousand. I don't know what the lower concentration of salt will do to me. I'm a sea* mammal, *you know.*

"I didn't know you *had* to live in salt water," Aleria said. "Aren't there freshwater porpoises and dolphins on Earth?"

*Yes, but they are not Orono. The Orono live in the sea.*

"So?"

*In fresh water, our skins become waterlogged. Our corneas cloud over.*

"Twenty-five parts per thousand is not exactly *fresh* water," Jemall observed. "As I recall, fresh water means less than one part salt per thousand."

*Yes, yes,* the dolphin replied irritably. *But I still don't know how the lower salt content will affect me. You'll have to monitor my condition at all times. I insist on it.*

"Oh, Lord, our dolphin's a hypochondriac." Aleria chuckled.

*There's no harm in being cautious,* Rosmer sniffed.

"That's true enough," the judge replied. "All right, Rossy old friend, we'll keep an eye on you."

The dolphin was only partially placated. *I don't like it when you make fun of me.*

"I wasn't making fun of you, Rossy. I was teasing."

*You're sure?*

Aleria stroked the wall of the tank, opening her mind to the dolphin to reveal the affection she bore him and her gratitude for his teaching her how to shield. "Don't you worry," she consoled him. "Everything will be fine once we land."

But now it was Houston's turn to be alarmed. "*Where am I supposed to land?*" he wanted to know. "There's only one island, Rix, and the transmissions indicate that it's sacred. I don't want to profane anybody's shrine, but I can't land in water, you know—not if you want me to be able to take off again."

This was a new wrinkle that Aleria hadn't considered. "Maybe . . . . Jemall, could you make him some kind of landing platform while we orbit?"

"Out of what?" the bailiff wanted to know.

"I don't know. Could you make it out of water? There seems to be an abundance of that down there."

*Can he really do that?* the dolphin demanded.

"Oh, sure." Aleria smiled. "He does it all the time. But I thought you said there was nothing new under the waves," she teased when she saw his excitement at the thought.

*Psionic matter transmutation—we've been trying it in the Rings Major for years. It's never worked. Oh, you must come and teach us how when we return to earth.*

Jemall's response was unusually modest. "To tell you the truth, I haven't got the entire technology down quite right. I was still working my way through the periodic table when I left school. I never did get to the heavier elements."

*Oh, then it's done according to formula!*

"Absolutely," replied the bailiff. "But I don't have all the formulae. I . . . dropped out of school before I completed my studies."

*What a shame. Still, you must teach us what you can.*

"As long as I don't have to go near the water," Jemall told him. "I don't like water." He shuddered. "I don't like this mission, either."

*So why are you here?*

"Orders," Jemall answered. "And Aleria."

"No telling tales out of school," Aleria cautioned.

*That's precisely what we hope to get him to do about the matter transmutation. But don't worry about his telling anything else. Your secrets are all still safe with me, Aleria. As I told you, it's a matter of Orono honor.*

"Well, okay," Aleria said. "But, listen, you two can't keep calling me by my first name when we get to Kahiko; it'll undermine my authority. From now on, you'd better refer to me as Your Honor or Judge."

Jemall smiled. "Okay, planet Kahiko, here come de judge."

"And here comes the planet Kahiko!" Houston announced. "Entering standard orbit about planet, awaiting further instructions."

"When you've got our orbit stabilized, let me know," the bailiff told him. "Then we can work on pulling the right formula out of your data banks to make that landing platform."

*I don't think that will be necessary*, Rosmer interjected. *The Kahikans know we're here—*

He broke off abruptly, and Aleria hastened to organize her mind into the augmentation mode they'd practiced. A message was coming through very clearly: *Welcome. We have waited for your return. We await you now on the sacred island.*

"Oh, damn," Aleria muttered aloud. "It sounds like one of those messages addressed to their gods. We can land, all right, but what're we going to do when they find out we're just mortals?"

"Don't tell 'em," Jemall suggested.

"That never works. They always find out, but in the meantime you wreck their culture. Oh, Lord, I feel like Cortez."

"Well, this does solve our landing problems," Jemall told her. "I wasn't sure I could create a platform."

"Jemall, this is serious. We may create a new mythos, along the lines of all those old Earth legends of gods from outer space," the judge pointed out. Then she sighed and added in a resigned tone, "I guess you're right. We have no choice. Houston, do you have landing coordinates for the island?"

"I do."

"Well, then, let's batten down the hatches and land."

"Okay," the ship replied. "Prepare for planetfall."

The judge and the bailiff checked the moorings on the dolphin's tank, then strapped themselves into their seats at the control console.

"Ready when you are," Aleria told Houston. "Let's go meet these mysterious Kahikans."

# Chapter IV

There really might be something to those legends about ancient space travelers seeding the planets with intelligent life, Aleria mused, watching through the viewer as Rix, the sole Kahikan island, grew from a pinpoint in the blue ocean to a substantial chunk of rock. One side of that rock was a broad, flat expanse that resembled a landing field. Its black basalt-like surface bore what appeared to be a five-pointed star at its center, made by inlaying paler, almost pink stone in the dark rock. A circle of reflective rocks marked the edge of the field and—on three sides—of the island itself. On those three sides, steep cliffs dropped almost vertically to the sparkling blue ocean below.

But on the fourth side, the island spread out in a broad semicircle that rose to form a small hill, then sloped gently down towards the sea. The hill was densely covered with foliage—vines, weeds, moss, and ferns—except for a broad path made of crushed shells, which led from the landing field to its crest. There, commanding a view of the sea from the highest point on the planet—all of three meters above sea level—stood a small arborlike building that appeared to have been carved out of pale pink coral, smoothed and burnished until it resembled rose-tinted marble.

"What's that supposed to be?" Jemall asked the judge.

"I don't know," she answered. "It could be a temple, considering the tenor of their welcoming broadcast. Or it could be the terminal building for their spaceport, complete with customs office and duty-free shop. Your guess is as good as mine." Then she added thoughtfully, "It does look as though they were expecting someone who would need a spaceport."

At this point, all conversation was cut off by the roar of Houston's engines as he reversed them, then rode their exhaust gently down, tail first, onto the five-pointed star in the middle of the field.

"We have probably just messed up the surface of their best tennis court," Aleria noted dryly. "Or perhaps this place was designed for use in their harvest festival, and we've just messed up the dance floor. Just because it *looks* like a landing field, and serves our purpose, doesn't mean it *is* one!"

"Now you tell me," Houston complained. "And after I've bolted myself onto their regulation class C mooring latches."

"Class C mooring latches?"

"There are class A, B, D, and E latches here as well, all imbedded at various appropriate points around the star."

Aleria was both relieved and alarmed. "Well, that means this isn't going to mark First Contact. I always hate that responsibility. But it may also mean that whoever has been here has been masquerading as a god from outer space. I don't like that one bit."

*Well, I don't like this tank one bit, so get me out of here,* Rosmer suggested.

"I thought you didn't trust the salinity of these waters," Jemall reminded him.

*It can't hurt for a short time, and I've got to get some exercise.*

"Okay," Aleria said. She and Jemall unfastened the bolts that held the top of the tank in place, wrapped the dolphin in damp spongecloth, and slipped a canvas stretcher underneath him. Using his service arms, Houston lifted the stretcher through the cargo bay doors as Aleria and Jemall scrambled through the passenger hatch and down the ladder, arriving just as Houston was about to set the dolphin down on the basalt surface.

Alarmed that lying on the ground might do Rosmer some injury, Aleria and Jemall each took one end of the stretcher and began to carry the heavy dolphin down the shell path toward the odd building and to the ocean beyond. They were almost at the small coral shelter when they got their first glimpse of the Kahikans, a small group of whom rose from the sea and walked slowly toward them with an odd, awkward gait.

"Rosmer," Aleria asked, "can you handle being a fish out of water just a little longer? I think we're about to meet our hosts."

*I guess I can, but try to get me into the shade of that building. If the sun dries out this spongecloth, I'm in bad trouble!*

Aleria nodded. She and Jemall and the dolphin kept their eyes fastened warily on the Kahikans; taking their cue from their hosts they, too, walked very slowly, though the burden of the dolphin seemed to increase with every measured step.

It wasn't until they reached the building that Aleria realized why the Kahikans had been moving so slowly. When they stood before her, she saw that the natives were powerfully built, with streamlined bodies tapering to a fine narrowness at the hip, and a slenderness at the ankles. But their feet fanned out like a frog's, though they walked like men. Aleria noticed that when the one who appeared to be their leader held up his hand in greeting, there was webbing between his fingers. She also noticed long red gill slits at the base of each Kahikan's neck. These were sealed, now, in the open air, and the Kahikans appeared to be mouth breathing like mammals. *True amphibians*, Aleria thought with surprise. Few animals on earth were able to adapt to water and land at the same stage of their development. Earth's amphibians were usually water dwellers first, land dwellers at maturity. The Kahikans were apparently both.

Their features bore this out. Their heads were human and fishlike at the same time, elongated, with flexible necks. Aleria guessed that when they swam, their faces pointed straight ahead, but here on land they bent their heads forward; the posture made them look very earnest, very curious.

But their colors were what really gripped Aleria's attention. The Kahikans seemed to be covered with an iridescent skin. On closer investigation, she could see that it was composed of fine, flat scales that gleamed beneath the Kahikan sun in every color of the rainbow, and some colors that she was sure had never been invented—pale greenish mauves, delicate coral pinks, and light tints of gold that verged on the paleness of platinum.

The Kahikans were not like any other humanoids Aleria had ever encountered—but they were certainly attractive. And they appeared to be naked except for scant costumes of fine netting, which draped them—males and females alike—from the right shoulder to just below the left hip. The loosely gathered costumes rose high on the right side to reveal well-muscled hips and even, on the taller natives, a glimpse of waist. The women, like the men, seemed unabashed at the exposure of the entire left side of their chests.

And they were mammalian, Aleria realized with some surprise. They were obviously able to suckle their young.

The netting looked fine enough not to hamper the Kahikans' movement in the water, but it surely wasn't designed for modesty. Aleria could easily visualize the costumes gently floating away from their wearers' bodies with every current—and, looking at the bodies of some of the Kahikan men, she liked the image very much.

The most remarkable characteristic of the costumes was their color, a brilliant, blinding crimson, more vibrant than any red Aleria had ever seen. It was a color that made her want to reach out and touch it. Though, with her red-gold hair and tawny skin, she usually avoided wearing red, Aleria knew at once that she wanted a judicial robe made of this netting—she could forgo the traditional black just this once—and she could almost feel Jemall's eagerness to deck himself out in Kahikan garb. Anyone who loved colors as much as Jemall did would probably be willing to kill for a costume created of that incredible red.

That thought reminded her of her mission here: The Kahikans might just be willing to kill for other reasons. Certainly, they were armed; they all wore, twisted into their net costumes just above the left hip, two carved quartz daggers, crossed to keep them in place like the decorative combs the geishas of ancient Japan had worn in their hair.

Aleria felt almost drab beside the brilliant Kahikans,

despite the sunshine that she knew brought out the gold in her coppery hair. She and Jemall had left the ship in ordinary white jumpsuits, since they had intended only to carry Rosmer to the water's edge, not to make contact with the Kahikans. As usual, Aleria wore her laser pistol strapped to one shapely thigh—she felt undressed without it—and Jemall wore his two Japanese swords suspended from a chartreuse-and-magenta sash. Rosmer's spongecloth wrapping obscured the brilliant white of his sides. Aleria was sure that the three of them presented a very dull image to the brilliant-hued Kahikans, and she hoped this wouldn't lower them in the natives' estimation.

Wishing she had worn her judicial robes which, by their very severity and utter blackness, lent her a certain dignity, she stepped forward and held up her hand, as had the Kahikan.

*We welcome you.* The Kahikan's message reverberated inside her skull. Well, at least there wouldn't be a translation problem; telepathy was nonverbal, even when one thought of it in terms of words as Aleria had just done.

Glancing at her companions, Aleria realized that the telepathic image had been as strong as Rosmer's conversation; even Jemall, who was telepathically deaf and dumb, had picked up on it.

The next image was more complex. The Kahikans requested that Aleria and her party bring their trade goods to the small shelter in which they now stood. The Kahikans expressed a particular interest in glass and mirrors.

"What do we do now?" Jemall wanted to know.

*We get me into the water*, Rosmer told him. *I'm very uncomfortable.*

This time the Kahikans picked up Rosmer's message and nodded in agreement. They stepped aside so that

Aleria and Jemall could lift the heavy stretcher once more and hasten to the sea with their dolphin friend. But there Jemall balked.

*Well?* demanded Rosmer impatiently. *Let's go.*

"No way," Jemall responded.

*I can't get in here*, the dolphin protested. *It's too shallow.*

"And I'm not going any farther," the bailiff told him bluntly. "It's too wet."

"While you two are arguing, my arms are breaking," Aleria complained. "Rosmer is no lightweight."

"I'm not going into that water," Jemall repeated.

"Then you're not going to be any use to me on Kahiko," Aleria growled. "Most of my fact-finding is going to take place in the water. I thought we'd settled this."

Jemall sighed. "You're right; we did."

"Well?" Aleria drummed her fingers impatiently on the handle of the stretcher. "You'll just have to adapt to the water."

"Gods, I hate the feel of that stuff, all slimy and *wet!*" Jemall shuddered.

"Frog," the judge reminded him.

"Frog?"

"You were going to turn into one."

Jemall nodded morosely. They set the dolphin down in the shallows, and the big silver bailiff began his preparations for transmuting himself. Aleria watched curiously. Jemall usually did this kind of thing in private, but the lack of available cover afforded Aleria an unusual opportunity to watch the bailiff exercise his shape-changing abilities.

Though he had some problems with complex molecules and the heavier metals, Jemall knew the composition of his own cells well enough to transmute them almost at will. Changing one's own cell structure was basic training in Acetan schools. But it was obvious to Aleria that Jemall was uncertain about something regarding this change, for he hesitated far longer than usual.

"Problem?" asked the judge.

"I'm not sure about the end product," he replied. "I might look like a frog and still hate the water."

"That shouldn't be a problem if you avoid turning toad."

"Toed?" Jemall looked down at his feet.

"That's not quite what I meant," Aleria giggled. "But if you're considering doing something to your feet, I'd suggest webbing."

*And you'd better change your scales from reptilian to fishy ones*, Rosmer added.

Jemall nodded morosely, then took a deep breath. He flexed his long, four-jointed fingers and began to mumble an incantation in his native tongue: "Oasti igthi easet rah nappipiens."

The transmutation was a rapid one, almost instantaneous. But Aleria, seizing this rare opportunity, watched intently, and managed to catch a glimpse of the change as it happened. It seemed to her that his skin actually crawled, just a bit, which made her own skin crawl in the figurative sense. She closed her eyes for a moment, and when she opened them again, Jemall stood transformed before her, now a huge, silver-scaled cross between an Acetan and a frog.

"Jem, you look terrific," she told him, bouncing over to kiss him on the cheek. His normally hot, dry skin felt slick and cool, and she started, then covered her reaction by snapping her fingers in mock disgust. "Darn, I thought you'd turn into a prince."

"I am a real prince of a fellow," he told her. "To prove it, I suggest we get our friend here into the water."

*Please do*, the dolphin said anxiously.

Taking up her end of the stretcher, Aleria watched in amusement as Jemall, took up the other end and tried the waters like a dubious bather on a cold September morn.

"Well?" Aleria demanded.

"I guess it's not bad," the bailiff conceded, "but, on the whole, I'd rather be in Philadelphia."

"Where the hell is Philadelphia?" Aleria asked him, baffled.

"Damned if I know," he said. "It's an expression I came across a few times while I was reading through Houston's data banks. I thought you'd know what it meant."

She shrugged. "I haven't a clue."

*Hey*, exclaimed the dolphin, *can we get on with this?*

"Sorry," Aleria and Jemall chimed in unison, and hastened into deeper waters. When they were waist deep in the surf, they floated the stretcher on the water's surface, removed the spongecloth, and let Rosmer roll off.

The dolphin heaved a great sigh of relief and began to dive beneath the waves, coming up for air and immediately going under again. Playfully, he sprayed the judge and the bailiff with sea water.

"Quit that," Aleria protested, mindful of the tendency of her long red hair to curl when it was dampened. But Jemall seemed delighted and began to frolic in the water beside the dolphin. Aleria noticed that the bailiff had given himself gill slits like the Kahikan's, so breathing underwater was not a problem for him.

"This feels great!" he shouted as he surfaced, then disappeared again beneath the waves, happily bouncing up and down in the water.

*Just wait until you try swimming*, Rosmer told him cheerily. *You'll love it; you'll probably keep your amphibious form for good.*

"I wouldn't bet on that," Jemall replied. "But there's a lot to be said for water when you're designed to function in it."

Aleria waited impatiently for them to finish frolicking and return to her. When at last they did, she reminded them of their purpose on Kahiko.

"What am I supposed to tell those guys up there on the hill?" she demanded. "For that matter, *how* am I supposed to talk to them without Rosmer?" she asked, for it had become quite obvious that the dolphin had no intention of leaving the sea in order to parlay with the Kahikans.

*Aw, you can do it yourself. They'll pick up your thoughts whenever you stop screening. Tell you what*, he offered. *If you want to bring them out here, I'll be glad to help you talk with them. If you want me for anything, just whistle.*

"You know I can't whistle under water like you can," Aleria protested.

*Sorry. Maybe you ought to have Jemall build that in when he transmutes you into an amphibian.*

It hadn't occurred to Aleria that Jemall was going to have to transmute her, too. Somehow, she had pictured herself neatly paddling along in scuba gear. She realized now that diving equipment would hamper her investigation, and that a transmutation was the most logical way to proceed.

Still, she didn't like the idea of the bai'ff messing around with her molecular structure. The last time he had tried that was when she had mentioned to him, quite casually, that she had always wanted a fur coat. He'd given her one that couldn't be removed—until he reversed his spell, and it had taken him several tries to get that right.

Having taken to water like a duck despite his former aversion to it, the bailiff, in his new form, was nowhere to be seen. Aleria trudged up the hill without him to where the Kahikans waited. She was muttering to herself about the uselessness of Orono and Acetans when she suddenly heard a strange *splotch, splotch* on the sandy beach behind her. Turning, she saw that great silver figure of Jemall plodding after her on newly webbed feet.

"I thought you were off having a frolic and detour," she told him sourly, using the legal term for those excursions from a business trip that were not considered part of it.

Jemall stared at her guilelessly.

"Hey, lady, it's my job to protect you." He put a reassuring arm around her shoulders.

"Nice of you to remember. But now I wish you'd remember that we aren't aboard the ship any longer. We have the dignity of the court to uphold." She smiled at him sweetly. "You remember the old adage that familiarity breeds contempt?"

He nodded.

"Well, remove your arm before I find you in contempt of court!"

"Right!" Jemall snapped, snatching the offending arm away and stepping smartly one pace to Aleria's rear.

"*What* has gotten into you?" Aleria demanded.

"Flies, I think."

"What?"

"Frogs eat them. Something that looked like a fly went by, and I ate it. I think it made me high." He grinned benignly.

"Try to sober up, would you?" Aleria pleaded. They were going to make a terrific first impression on the Kahikans, she told herself sarcastically. It might be better to masquerade as a trading party—if Jemall could manage to sober up long enough to convert some of Houston's extraneous equipment and stores to trade goods. Feeling less than impressive, Aleria squared her shoulders and marched with as much dignity as she could muster into the colonnaded shelter to confront the natives once more.

"We come in peace," she was just starting to announce, when suddenly the Kahikans moved forward in a mighty surge—toward Jemall! The males prostrated themselves before him, pressing their foreheads into the sand, and the half a dozen females in the party threw themselves supine onto the sand before him, mouths open and legs spread wide, in very obvious invitation.

Jemall was not one to miss such a signal. His body responded as only an Acetan's could, his large organ growing immense beneath his tight-fitting white jumpsuit which, wet from the ocean, now clung to him more snugly than ever, revealing every detail of his response. Witnessing his reaction, the Kahikans sighed audibly, the men groveling with their bare bottoms elevated toward the wide gray skies, and the women now lifting their hips in an even more blatant invitation.

Jemall grinned happily at the sexual surfeit exhibited before him, but Aleria, shocked, voiced a demand for an explanation before she had a chance to think better of it. "What in this wet world is going on?"

The Kahikans' telepathic reply, sent, as it was, in chorus, nearly bowled her over with its force. The image it depicted was unmistakable and, when Aleria stopped to think about it, extremely funny. Jemall had inadvertently given himself the shape of one of their gods—the Kahikan equivalent of Priapus, ancient god of procreation! The telepathic image Aleria had received was that of a great silver frog, enormously and inexhaustibly endowed—and, glancing at her bailiff, she realized that he fit that image in almost every detail.

They were about to be stuck with the sobriquet of gods from outer space whether they liked it or not. Aleria glanced again at the bailiff, and saw that he was stripping off his jumpsuit in order to oblige the nearest Kahikan female. Under normal circumstances, the judge would have abjured any circumscription of the big bailiff's activities, sexual or otherwise, but servicing the entire welcoming party—which, she knew from experience, Jemall could manage—was just not her idea of the most appropriate manner in which to initiate Confederation contact with Kahiko.

"Jemall!" she called out sharply. The commanding tone of her voice managed to penetrate his befogged mind, and he stopped his advance and pulled his jumpsuit back up over his straining silver appendage.

"Sorry," he mumbled.

The Kahikans, though disappointed, were obviously impressed. There was no red-haired goddess in their pantheon, but anyone who could command this personification of the frog god was undoubtedly worthy of worship. Now they bowed before her, too, sending telepathic messages of awe and respect.

*We accept your respect but not your worship*, Aleria told them firmly but kindly. *We are not gods, but representatives of a distant government that rules many planets.*

The Kahikan leader, who had scrambled to his feet when Jemall acceded to Aleria's command, now looked up sharply. *You are from the Confederation of Planets.*

Aleria nodded, taken aback. *How did you know about the Confederation?* she asked.

*The traders for whom we built this port on our only island told us of the great Confederation. We have seen your products, and our people covet them.* Here Aleria suddenly received a strong telepathic vision of mirrors, glass bottles, and smoothly formed metal and plastic objects. *We wish to join your Confederation*, the Kahikan said bluntly.

This was a new wrinkle, but one that could solve her problems of access to evidence, Aleria realized. If she were authorized to investigate this planet for admission to the Confederation, she could search for the source of the mysterious message at the same time. If it proved false, she could certify the planet for admission. In fact, if the Kahikans actually practiced genocide of intelligent life forms, then admission might be in order anyway; the Confederation would then be empowered to step in and stop them.

But was she empowered to make such an investigation? Aleria doubted it.

*I will have to consult the Confederation to see if I have the authority to rule on your request*, she told the Kahikan. *While I do so, you might want to draw up a formal petition for admission, in the name of all intelligent species on this planet.*

*Petition?* asked the Kahikan.

*Give us your reasons for wanting to join, a bit of your history, your previous Confederation contacts, and tell us a little about Kahiko—what you have to trade, how you live, what you seek.*

*We will do that*, the Kahikan told her. *But first, couldn't we—?* He glanced appealingly at Jemall.

But the big bailiff, now sober, only shook his head.

*No*, Aleria answered for him, not unkindly. *At another time and place, perhaps. Right now, we have to send a message back to Confederation headquarters. You'll excuse us?*

The Kahikans did so reluctantly. They began to retreat toward the sea, all the while casting hungry glances at Jemall.

"Couldn't we——?" he began.

"Not a good idea before we've been briefed on their customs," Aleria noted. "There are cultures with traditions that could make you worse than uncomfortable—like the mantis men of Microscopium, who devour their partners after sexual intercouse. *We* speak of 'eating,' but we don't mean it literally. They *do!*"

Jemall nodded. Aleria knew he had read of Gamma Microscopium 3, the planet of which she had spoken, not to mention the fatal stings imparted to unwary travelers who tried to mate with the natives of Girtab 7. It was all in Houston's data banks, which Jemall searched voraciously during their long voyages through the great void. The tales were fascinating, if sometimes horrifying; interstellar intercourse had given new meaning the term *venereal disease*, not the least contribution to which was the only truly *venereal* disease, Venusian ringworm. Still, the Kahikans did not appear to be dangerous, deranged, or diseased, and Jemall was not one to pass up an opportunity without a protest.

"Surely you don't think the Kahikans——" he began, but Aleria cut him off.

"We have no planet surveys to go by, and Houston hasn't even scanned the place or the inhabitants, other than a preliminary scan to see if the air was breathable and the surface nontoxic. And don't forget, we are here to investigate allegations of genocide," she reminded him.

Jemall didn't scare that easily. "It would have been nice. One seldom has so many opportunities at once."

"I didn't realize you felt there was a shortage of opportunities," Aleria told him archly.

Jemall merely shrugged. "It's been a long time."

Aleria was forced to concede that point. Having a porpoise as a passenger had cramped not only their quarters but also their style. "But Rosmer's gone to sea," she cajoled. "We could dismantle his tank. That would give us back our main cabin."

Jemall was not one to ignore such an attractive suggestion. He and Aleria had come to regard Houston's main cabin as their own private pleasure palace. They normally passed the time on the long interstellar voyages between stops on Aleria's circuit by reading the erotic literature of the Confederation's many worlds (which included some tricks that had never existed except in the minds of their creators), and by enacting scenes that interested them, as the spirit moved them—and as Jemall's transmutation abilities allowed. But with Rosmer's tank filling their playground and with his testy presence filling their lives, Aleria and Jemall hadn't had so much as an ordinary coupling since their visit to the golden sand beach from which Houston had summoned them for this mission.

"Tell you what," said the bailiff, poising himself to try his new frog legs. "I'll race you back to Houston for the right to choose today's game." With one mighty bound he had far outdistanced her, but this was one contest the flame-haired judge didn't mind losing, for the real prize was Jemall himself. That prize awaited her back on the ship.

The very thought of what awaited her caused that old familiar melting sensation in her lower abdomen. Before it could reach her knees and slow her down, she lengthened her stride and fairly flew the remaining distance across the island to the landing field. Obtaining the authorization to pass on Kahiko's admission to the Confederation could take some time. Judge Aleria Farrell had a really good idea of how she intended to fill those waiting hours.

# Chapter V

Houston hated waiting. It struck him as a form of down time, and like any conscientious machine, he abhorred down time.

"I don't see why we can't go ahead with your original mission and investigate that appeal for assistance," he complained to Aleria.

"It's simple. Kahiko isn't a member of the Confederation. If I find that an intelligent race is being slaughtered, the most I can do is ask the Confederation to censure the Kahikans. That won't help the victims much."

"The Confederation could place a trade embargo on Kahiko," Houston suggested.

Jemall snorted derisively.

Aleria was more patient. "A trade embargo wouldn't be very effective. Rogue traders obviously made First Contact without Confederation authority. Kahiko is so far off the beaten track that you can't expect to enforce an embargo. Besides, they could question the legality of my evidence if I obtain it under false pretenses. But if I'm inspecting conditions here to determine Kahikan eligibility to join the Confederation, anything I turn up is fair game."

So Houston had dutifully sent off Aleria's request for authorization to evaluate Kahiko for admission. Then he had also dutifully blocked his monitors in the main cabin, giving the judge the privacy that she and the bailiff had demanded.

Aleria and Jemall took their own sweet time about emerging, but the reply from Judicial Central took even longer.

It couldn't be helped. Message transmission, like any other form of space travel, was governed by the laws of physics. Messages traveled at the speed of sound or the speed of light unless you sent them through a space-and-time warp. The problem with that, Houston reminded himself morosely, was that you couldn't just send a signal through a warp; if you did, it bounced back and forth in the warp, bent backward, and sometimes even turned itself inside out. It inevitably came out bearing no resemblance to its original form, not unlike the whispered messages in that children's game where a phrase was whispered from one child to another just to see how garbled it could become.

A message sent through a warp had to be sent in a drone container, so message transmission took almost as long as space travel itself. That was why Houston now stood on the landing field at Rix, doing what everybody did when they came to Rix. He waited. And waited. And waited.

It would have been so much simpler, he reflected glumly, if he could have sent a telepathic message. Telepathic messages defied the laws of space and time, whisking instantly from one end of the known universe to the other.

But for a mechanical being like Houston, telepathic contact was possible only with persons whose transponders were attuned to his mind. There were only two such persons in the universe right now, Aleria and Jemall. Judge Ashippun's transponder had been removed when he moved up to the Court of Appeals. Though Houston was also keyed to a dispatch station at the edge of Aleria's circuit, since Kahiko lay in the opposite direction across the galaxy, a message sent via the dispatch station would have had to travel so far that the diffusion factor would have caused too much distortion.

Besides, the dispatch station was a busybody. Houston tried to convey as little as possible through that station, for anything you told it tended to end up common knowledge along the spaceways.

"Someday," the ship consoled himself, "we'll solve these communications problems." Maybe not in Aleria's lifetime, or Jemall's, but a machine that was well tended would last a lot longer than the normal human "ten score and three."

Bored, Houston glanced at the horizon, where nothing much was happening. " 'Water, water everywhere,' " he quoted the ancient poet, Coleridge, to himself. " 'As idle as a painted ship upon a painted ocean.' " Then he perked up. The leader of the Kahikans had risen from the sea and was coming down the crushed-shell path toward the landing field. The Kahikan probably meant trouble, but trouble was better than boredom, better than waiting for word from the warp.

Levis Ostego passed all his days waiting for word from the warp. It had been almost a month since that mysterious message had come in over the sublim. The Ring Minor had convened, and one of its dolphins had even gone off with the investigating team. But Levis was still here, monitoring, and more bored than ever.

His intercom sounded, a call from Garcia, one of the patrol pilots who made mail pickups on the warp catchers.

"Ostego here. What've you got?" Levis asked him.

"Drone from someplace called Kahiko."

"Kahiko? Never heard of it."

"It's marked 'Priority: Judicial Central.' It's addressed to a Judge Ashippun, from a Judge Farrell."

That was the judge who had gone off to investigate the sublim's alarm! "Bring it on in, Garcia—by the day before yesterday!"

"Right. I'm on it."

Levis switched to Medina's circuit. "Just got a message from Garcia," he told her. "He's bringing in a drone from the judge who's investigating that sublim alarm we picked up."

"Get it on the deciphering machine as soon as it comes in," his supervisor told him. "I'll be right there."

Levis nodded. "Should I summon the dolphins?" He liked the three dolphins who'd remained on the station, even though their bright presence made him feel a bit like a dullard.

"No," Medina told him, "let's wait to see if we need them. They make me feel inferior, with all their telepathic ability. There seems to be almost nothing they can't do."

"They can't type," Levis reminded her.

Medina laughed pleasantly. "Neither can I. But let's see if I can figure out this message without their assistance."

The Kahikan approached and raised his hand in greeting. "Hail, golden Houston. It is I, Nehinei."

"Yes," said the ship. "I recognize you."

"Oh, I'm so pleased," Nehinei replied. "The traders who came before never knew who I was. They said we all looked alike."

"They must, at the very least, have been colorblind," Houston commented dryly. "Even if your features were identical, no two of you are the same color. Anyway, you're the only one who speaks Confederation Standard."

"The traders taught us all. My companions do not enjoy making sounds with their throats. But I enjoy communicating. I practice for the time when the traders return. When I am able to communicate well, I will trade well." He looked up at the ship's speakers, from which Houston's voice had come, and smiled. "The traders were not very bright. They gave us many objects of glass, and we merely gave them some of our red robing—a small price to pay for so great a treasure as glass."

"If you say so." Houston yawned. "Nehinei, why do the Kahikans value glass so highly? It isn't worth very much to the people of the other planets. Some worlds even have a problem disposing of it, because so much is manufactured; it's usually just thrown away."

"Thrown away? *Thrown away! Glass?*" Nehinei demanded. "Who would be so wasteful?"

"One man's trash is another man's treasure."

"But glass! It's so hard to come by, so crystal clear, like the frozen waters of the polar region, but it doesn't melt. You can trap air inside it and it will float. Was there ever anything more marvelous?"

"I can think of a few things," Houston remarked. "I can't understand why you don't make your own glass. I've scanned Kahiko, and I know you have plenty of silica in your sand. You also have lime and potash and lead. Making glass is no big deal."

"It isn't?" Nehinei looked doubtful.

"No, of course not. Just melt the sand—"

"Melt? *Sand*? Impossible."

"No, it isn't. Just fan your flames—"

"Flames?" asked Nehinei. "What are flames?"

Houston sighed. "Nehinei, I am about to open up vistas for you that you have never even dreamed of on this water world. You're missing one of the basic elements. Have I got a surprise for you!"

Levis and Medina put the message through to Judge Ashippun by radio beam and were not surprised when his reply was almost instantaneous.

"Of course Aleria can have the authority to rule on admission to the Confederation. I've polled my colleagues, and they agree completely. This will put her in a much stronger position to enforce her rules. Please get word to her at once."

"Yes, sir," Levis replied. "But bear in mind that it took nearly two weeks for her message to get here, and it will take just as long for this one to reach Kahiko." Even as he spoke, the young technician was preparing Judge Ashippun's message for transmission by drone.

"Can't you send it any faster?" the judge asked him.

"Not without breaking the laws of physics—and they're a lot harder to break than the laws you work with."

The old judge nodded. "Well, do your best."

His image vanished from the video screen.

"*Are* we doing our best?" Levis asked Medina as they stuffed the drone into the pneumatic tube that would take it to Garcia.

"What do you mean?" she asked. "You know as well as I do that there is no other way."

"But there *is* !"

"Telepathy?" Medina asked. "We'd need a telesend and a receiver. Where—"

"The dolphins," Levis told her.

"The dolphins?"

"We have three. And the one with Judge Farrell was supposed to teach her how to augment—"

"You're right. Let's find the dolphins!" Medina grabbed Levis by the arm, and the two of them were off and running down the corridor to the tank where the three dolphins awaited Rosmer's return to their Ring.

*It can't be done*, Selmar narrowcast at them. *We are only three. We need four for the power of a Ring, even a Ring Minor.*

"Rosmer's all by himself, with just Judge Farrell. You expect *her* to augment him enough to find the sender of that message?" Levis protested.

*Judge Farrell is a sensitive*, Selmar reminded him.

"So are we—sort of."

The dolphins looked at Levis and Medina apprizingly, as though taking their measure.

*Maybe we could*, Carswell ventured.

*It might work*, Selmar allowed, *especially if Judge Farrell and Rosmer are augmenting when we send. If they are, they should pick up any stray messages.*

*We should be able to contact Rosmer, anyway, because he's part of our Ring*. Sebrook pointed out. *We're attuned to him, and he to us.*

Selmar still had reservations. *It's an awfully long distance, and we don't know where on Kahiko they are. No matter how constricted we keep the beam, it's going to have to blanket the planet. The message could be so diffuse as to be unintelligible.*

"Let's take the chance," Medina encouraged. "How often does a Ring have a receiver at the other end of so long a transmission? If it works, we'll go down in history."

The dolphins gave the equivalent of a shrug.

*One crash course in augmentation coming up,* said Selmar. He instructed Levis and Medina to lean against the tank, and the lessons began.

Nehinei's lessons in scholastic philosophy were proving an amusement to Houston. The Kahikan understood that air and earth—he called them *lahnee* and *lepoh*—could be as important, or *almost* as important, as water, which he called *sagara*.

"After all," he pointed out to the ship, "the lepoh blankets the great sea from beneath, and the lahnee blankets it from above. To the creatures who cling to the floor of the sea, and those, like my people, who can live on its surface, these edges of the world are important. But there can be no more elements, as you call them. There are moods, of course—light and darkness, cold and warmth—but though they affect air and earth and water, they are not equal to them."

"An interesting way to look at it, and not unlike the way the ancient philosophers of Earth did," Houston noted. "But you should know there are more things in heaven and earth, Nehinei, than are dreamt of in your philosophy."

Houston heard a familiar chuckle and realized that the privacy switch on his cabin monitors had been lifted, admitting Aleria and Jemall to the conversation. "Did you find something amusing, Your Honor?" he asked.

"Just that I hope you're not going to claim credit for that line. It's been around awhile."

"I know that." The ship was annoyed. "I was just trying to find a dramatic enough way to introduce Nehinei, here, to the concept of fire."

"It won't do you much good to play Prometheus here — there's nothing combustible on this entire planet. What's he going to burn?"

"He's got a thing for glass. And there's plenty of silica here. So I merely thought I'd show him how to use solar power, and that glass he likes so much, to make other glass." At this, Houston produced a magnifying lens.

Nehinei, who had been totally baffled by Houston's conversation with a disembodied female voice, saw the magnifying glass and reached out for it curiously. Houston decided to let him play with it while the two of them waited for Aleria and Jemall to emerge.

When they did, it was apparent that Aleria had been transformed. She jumped from the hatch, eschewing the use of the ladder, and landed lightly on newly webbed feet. New powerful and supple muscles had been incorporated into her long legs, which nevertheless had retained their shapeliness. Aleria was vain enough to have insisted on that, Houston reflected. She also had gill slits now, which, like those of the Kahikans, could be sealed in the open air.

She bounded over to where Nehinei, peering curiously through the magnifying glass, was about to inspect the Kahikan sky. It was one of those rare periods when there was an opening in the great high banks of clouds, and the pale gold Kahikan sunlight streamed down upon them. Aleria snatched the glass from Nehinei's long, webbed fingers before he could squint through it.

"Watch it," she told him, alarm in her voice. "You could burn your eyes out."

"Burn?" Nehinei asked, turning his great bluish green eyes to her in obvious puzzlement. "I do not understand your meaning."

"Houston will show you." It was an order. She turned to face the ship and added, "If they're going to trade with the Confederation, they'd better know about fire. But show them the dangers, too, Prometheus, or you'll lose your liver."

"No need to get nasty," the ship replied. "Anyway, I don't have a liver."

"That omission can be rectified," Jemall told him ominously.

*What good could a liver possibly do a ship?* Houston wondered. *I'd probably get cirrhosis from my own rocket fuel.* But he set about assembling some sand containing the necessary elements, then took the magnifying glass and focused the rays of the Kahikan sun, now at its zenith, on the small mound. He turned the glass to obtain maximum concentration, and gradually the amplified sunlight melted the sand into a froth of fragile, grayish bubbles. These were opaque and thinner than paper, but still recognizable as glass.

"So glass is manufactured, not mined!" Nehinei sat back on his haunches, looking very satisfied. "Then, with the right glass, we can *make* glass."

"Well, that's one of the ways to do it," Jemall told him. "I do it this way." And he flexed his magic fingers and muttered something under his breath. The pile of brittle gray shards became a fine crystalline bauble, at once both intricate and simple in its alien design.

"Why, Jemall, you're an artist!" Aleria exclaimed. "That's beautiful."

"It is," said Nehinei, "but what it tells me is that we were correct: you *are* the personification of Pipiens, the frog god."

"No," Jemall assured him, "it's merely a skill I've learned over the years. You can't do it my way, but you can seek the help of your sun. Most of its light is just sitting there, waiting to be used."

"This was fire?" asked Nehinei, gesturing toward the magnifying glass.

"Of a sort. *This* is true fire," said the Acetan, and, transmuting a bit of leftover sand into a lump of charcoal, he set it ablaze, right there on the basalt landing field.

Nehinei reached out toward it. Jemall was about to stop him, but Aleria grabbed the bailiff's arm, stopping him in mid-gesture.

"No," she whispered. "Let him. He won't believe us otherwise."

Nehinei let out a yelp and snatched back his scorched fingers, putting them, in an apparently universal gesture, into his mouth.

"The burned child shuns the fire," the judge whispered to Jemall. "Tell your people," she told the Kahikan.

He turned to her in dismay and wonder, and nodded. "I shall convey it."

"When he tells it telepathically, it will be as though they all had experienced it," Aleria explained to Houston and Jemall.

"So it will," Nehinei affirmed. "Nothing experienced by any one of us need ever be alien to the rest."

Then he looked again at the burning charcoal. "But this," he said, "this is something the like of which I never dreamed of, not even in my wildest fantasies deep in the throes of *sumati*. I pictured other worlds, but never such a thing as fire."

"You pictured other worlds?" Aleria was curious about that and about his reference to *the throes of sumati*. "Why? How?"

"We know there must be something beyond. We feel messages from the other side of the great blanket of lahnee, where the clouds sail and the sun sometimes appears. We have legends of other seas, of different fish, of wonders unknown to us."

" 'Wetter water, slimier slime,' " Aleria quoted.

"Exactly!" exclaimed Nehinei.

"Was that Rupert Brooke?" Houston asked.

"Yes," replied Aleria. "A fish's concept of heaven. It's a poem," she explained to Jemall. "Centuries old. Houston will show it to you."

"When do I get to show you the wonders of my world?" Nehinei asked her, and there was an odd extra promise in his tone that even Houston could recognize.

"Soon," Aleria told him absently, looking toward the sky, "Soon. We are waiting for one of those messages you spoke of, words from beyond your sun." Then she turned to the Kahikan and smiled flirtatiously. "Could I persuade you to find my dolphin friend who is somewhere in your great sea?"

"The one they call Rosmer?"

"That's him."

"First I must tell my people of fire. Then I will summon him to you."

"Thanks," said Aleria. "I can't seem to reach him. I think he doesn't want to be reached."

Nehinei nodded. "I will reach him," he promised. "He will come."

# Chapter VI

It was an idyllic picture—Aleria and Jemall lolling lazily in the shallows, Rosmer swimming up to bask beside them, then sounding in the offshore depths and returning to the beach once more.

Far above them, the high white clouds floated just as lazily. Behind them lay the coral colonnade of the only surface structure on Kahiko, while behind that rose the gleaming gold-and-white shaft that was Houston.

The waters lapped lazily at the shining sands, and beneath their surface, graceful weeds undulated with the gentle movement of the ocean currents. On this lazy afternoon, even the fish that normally darted to and fro beneath the waves floated tranquilly, suspended in the crystalline sea.

Aleria hummed a folk tune she'd learned as a child, the song of an island in the sun, with sparkling waters and shining sands, as she listened to the lapping of the waves and the occasional splash of a flying fish leaving or reentering the waters. She watched the horizon through hooded eyes as a pair of much larger splashes indicated that the "fish" breaking the surface was Rosmer.

The dolphin had been oddly evasive about his activities during his prolonged absence from Rix. She meant to pin him down to specifics the next time he rolled into the shallows. But later; there was time.

The narrowcast from earth hit the highly sensitive inhabitants of Kahiko like a lighting bolt. Nehinei, who had been effusively expressing his delight over Houston's gift to him of a waterproof flashlight—cool fire in a container, he called it—froze where he stood. The various denizens of the deep heard it, too. The lazy afternoon became charged with wariness; everyone was instantly alert.

But only Rosmer and Aleria, at whom it was aimed, understood it. For the image sent across the great void of space was of Justice holding her scales in one hand and lifting her blindfold with the other in order to peer at a small fish. Telepathy was nonverbal, and the single image that could be sent this far had to convey everything in one instantaneous mental picture.

This one had done so. Aleria knew, without it having been verbalized, that she had been granted the authority she had sought. But how had it reached her?

Rosmer knew. He shot from the waves in a giant arc, whistling shrilly in his excitement and narrowcasting to Aleria at the same time, *The Ring! My Ring! They've reached me across the light years that lie between us—my Ring, my Ring.*

If a dolphin could have wept for joy, Rosmer would have done so. Until that very moment, Aleria had not realized the loneliness he was suffering at being separated from his Ring.

"Can we answer them?" she asked him.

*I don't think so*, he replied cautiously, but with more than a hint of longing in his tone. *There are three of them, and someone or something else is augmenting.* He skittered backward along the crests of the waves on his tail, then plunged beneath the surface and came up as near to Aleria as he could without beaching himself.

"We can augment," Aleria pointed out.

*Only enough to communicate here on this planet, not enough to send word across the great void.*

"Oh," Aleria said, disappointed. Then she brightened. "The Kahikans are telepaths. Could they learn to augment?"

Rosmer pondered a moment. *I suppose they could, although discipline isn't in their nature. But I think we ought to wait to see if they can be trusted before we turn them on to interstellar interchanges.*

"You don't trust them?" Aleria exclaimed in surprise.

*I didn't say that. But—*

"But what?"

*They may have different values. Isn't that what we're here to investigate?*

"Of course."

His telepathic voice diminished to the thinnest of narrowcasts, which only Aleria could read, and she just barely. *Then don't let them know yet how great their powers might be until we're sure of them. Send a drone.* Rosmer managed to convey such regret in that last order that Aleria understood what it cost him to be out of touch with his Ring and what discipline he was exercising by urging restraint.

"I'll do that," she said and sprang up the beach in newly-mastered froggy leaps all the way to the landing pad. "Houston," she told the ship, "send a drone back through the warp: 'Telepathic authorization received. Proceeding to investigate Kahiko for admission to Confederation.' "

"What authorization?" the ship demanded.

"Rosmer's ring contacted us."

"I didn't hear anything."

"You're not a telepath," Aleria pointed out.

"I am when you use your transponder."

"It gives me a headache; you know that. Funny," she added thoughtfully, "mental telepathy, without the transponder, doesn't bother me at all."

"Well, what's all this about?" Houston asked her, as he dutifully launched the tiny drone.

"We have a go-ahead." Aleria turned to face Nehinei, who had been standing, still frozen by the force of the Ring's message, at the edge of the launching pad. "I am authorized to inspect conditions on Kahiko and rule on your petition to join the Confederation. Will you arrange for a guide?"

"It would be my pleasure to show you the wonders of Kahiko myself," Nehinei told her.

Aleria thought she heard something suggestive in that statement, but she let it pass. Perhaps it was only her imagination. "I'll also need a hearing room, someplace where I can take testimony from anyone wishing to argue for or against admission and make my ruling."

"We can provide that," Nehinei told her. "We have such a place."

"Well, let's get on with it," Aleria said. "We've waited around Rix long enough."

"This way is quickest," Nehinei told her and, threading the stem of the flashlight through the red netting he wore draped across his torso, he gave a great froglike leap off the edge of the flat basalt spaceport into the clear blue-green waters that lapped at the base of the miniature cliffs that formed its shore.

Aleria looked cautiously over the edge. The cliffs were barely three meters above the water level, but the sea at that point seemed at least as deep. She glanced down at herself. She was wearing a silver string bikini, more string than bikini, but it served to hold her laser pistol, which she had thrust through the strings that looped over her narrow hips. Another silver cord, tied about her forehead, would keep her flowing red hair out of her eyes. She guessed she was as ready as she'd ever be.

She poised for her own froglike leap into the depths, then stopped. There ought to be some appropriate phrase for an action like this. She remembered an ancient video about two outlaws on Earth who had made a great jump from a cliff into a river. One of them, she recalled, had hollered an extended obscenity. She shook her head. That wasn't how she wanted her entrance to the Kahikan waters to be marked. Then it came to her.

Springing from the cliff in a graceful leap, she sailed toward the waters shouting an ancient war cry: "Geronimo!"

Whatever that meant.

Aleria's first discovery about the undersea world was that, despite Jemall's modifications, she was not designed to be an underwater creature.

It wasn't the fault of her gills; they functioned just fine, opening automatically the moment she submerged. She felt a pleasant, almost erotic sensation as the waters slipped through them, a feeling halfway between a tickle and an electric shock.

Jemall had even given her eyes an extra lid, a thin membrane that covered them automatically when she sank beneath the waves. This made it possible for her to see under water as well as she did on land, although the translucent eyelids acted like a pair of pink sunglasses. Looking at the underwater world through rose-colored glasses was not her intention, especially since she was on a fact-finding mission. She blinked several times in an attempt to correct the color distortion, then decided that Jemall would just have to adjust it with the same transmutation he had used to create it—and with all due haste. Aleria was sure she find the rosy glow that it imparted extremely annoying in time.

Unfortunately, she was finding her own buoyancy even more annoying. She couldn't manage to spend enough time under water to get a good look—even a rosy one—at anything. In fact, no sooner had her feet lightly touched the ocean floor than she shot upward again in a cascade of bubbles and found herself floating on the surface of the sea.

"Hey," she complained to no one in particular, "this isn't working." Deciding that her precipitous expulsion from the underwater world might have been just the rebound from her forceful, feet-first entry into it, she attempted a long, arcing surface dive to take her back to the bottom at a more gentle angle.

This time she managed to stay down almost a full minute before a force beyond her control drew her, face first, back to the surface.

Aleria remained there awhile, treading water and considering what might have gone wrong. She concluded that it had been her attempt to stand upright on the sea bottom. Fish, after all—except for the sea horse—swam in a horizontal position.

She entered the depths again, this time remaining horizontal and propelling herself along by pushing the water behind her with powerful strokes of her lean, strong arms. She enjoyed the sensation of the water against the fine finger webbing Jemall had given her by transmuting some of the skin on her hands. The warm water slid sensuously across those panels of translucent skin, and she concentrated on the sensation, letting her slender legs just trail behind her.

But again she found herself drifting toward the surface. She realized that she was expending almost as much energy staying down as going forward. Giving a series of determined kicks with her newly-altered legs, she managed to keep herself beneath the surface, but only as long as she remained in motion. The moment she relaxed, she found herself shooting upward once again.

Just before she broke through the shimmering surface for the fourth time, Aleria became aware of a gallery of giggles. Her struggle to stay beneath the waves was being watched, and with amusement, by the denizens of the deep.

Annoyed, she circled the island with quick, powerful arm strokes. On the beach side of Rix, Jemall was waiting in the shallows.

"What's up?" he asked her innocently as she strode up the sloping beach.

"*I* seem to be."

"Huh?"

"I can't stay down. I keep bobbing to the surface. And everything looks pink through these extra eyelids you gave me."

"I can fix the eyelid problem," he informed her casually and flexed his fingers at her. She could feel something happening to her eyes. She consciously forced the extra eyelid down. Sure enough, her vision was now as clear as a crystal.

"One problem fixed," she told Jemall. "Now, about my tendency to float . . . ."

Jemall shrugged. "Maybe you're doing something wrong."

"I doubt it." Aleria wrinkled her nose petulantly. "And we're not going anywhere until you figure out why I keep surfacing."

*Fat*, Rosmer announced, coming up behind her suddenly in the water.

"What?" Aleria jumped, startled at the sudden mental intrusion.

*Fat*, the dolphin repeated.

"I am not," Aleria protested. She looked down at her curvaceous body. She tended to be a bit wide of shoulder, but she was slender of waist and narrow of hip. "I am not!" she repeated emphatically.

"I'm afraid you are, although it isn't a fat *I'd* object to," Nehinei noted as came up beside the dolphin.

The four of them squared off there, hip deep in the shallow water. Aleria stood with her hands on her hips, glaring at Rosmer and Nehinei defiantly, while Jemall, who knew the judge's temper well, tried—very awkwardly due to his flipperlike feet—to back discreetly up the sloping sand beach.

*It's a problem most sea mammals have*, Rosmer explained placatingly. *Specific gravity brings us to the surface. And your—fat—just isn't positioned right for streamlined swimming.*

Aleria was puzzled. "Whatever are you talking about?"

"This," said Nehinei. He surprised her by striding up to her, and cupping his hand gently around her breast.

It was the kind of innocent gesture that, as a primitive, he could *almost* get away with—but Aleria knew he was copping a feel. He had had just a bit too much suggestion in his voice when he had spoken earlier of showing her "the wonders of Kahiko." She suspected that some of those wonders were parts of his own anatomy. However, she liked his light touch, the odd feel of his alien fingers. She decided not to take offense.

"Oh," she remarked, removing Nehinei's hand gently with both of her own. She held it just a moment longer than was necessary before letting it go. "Well, what do we do about my 'fat' problem?"

The Kahikan and the dolphin looked to Jemall for an answer.

"I suppose I could transmute them," he said cautiously.

Aleria suddenly remembered that the Kahikan females were comparatively flat-chested, and realized just what Jemall was suggesting. She was as vain about her firm, rounded breasts as she was about the rest of her body. "Nothing doing, Buster," she told him.

"I don't know how else to solve the problem." Jemall shook his head.

There was a dead silence for a moment.

*Back on earth, divers often wear weights*, Rosmer ventured.

"That's it!" Aleria beamed. "Jemall, just make me a weight belt. Something heavy—and pretty!"

"Find me something to make it *out* of," Jemall told her petulantly.

She knew he didn't like producing psionic matter transmutations on demand, but there didn't seem to be any alternatives here on Kahiko, where fire and all forms of manufacturing that stemmed from the use of it were unknown. She decided that her safest course was to ignore his unvoiced complaint.

"We'll find *something*," she smiled brightly. But as she glanced about beach, she realized that nothing seemed readily available.

She looked at the others helplessly. Rosmer and Nehinei met each other's eyes, then quickly disappeared beneath the waves. They returned after a moment or two bearing several odd Kahikan rocks, with shiny veins of metal running through them. Nehinei carried a number of them in his webbed hands, and Rosmer carried one smaller one in his mouth.

"Will these do?" asked Nehinei.

Jemall brightened. "Yeah, they will. They're perfect!"

He flexed his long Acetan fingers and concentrated, and the rocks seemed to writhe on the sand before them. Seconds later, a belt of rough gold lumps lay on the beach where the rocks had been.

"How's that?" the bailiff asked proudly.

"Nope," said Aleria.

"What's wrong with it?" he demanded.

"First," Aleria told him, "those nuggets are rough. They'll be uncomfortable to wear."

"Oh," said Jemall. "Well, I can fix that." He flexed his fingers again, and the rough lumps became a series of oblong beads, still gold—but the gold now had a greenish cast to it. His spells tended to go at least a little awry more often than not. The greenish tint of the golden beads was par for the course.

But Aleria still was not happy. "You didn't give me a chance to finish what I was saying," she told him.

"Uh-oh," Jemall muttered under his breath. "Okay, let's have it."

"I'm wearing silver. Gold will clash—especially that awful greenish gold."

Jemall nodded. Aleria was not to be put off when she set her mind on something; he knew that, and she knew he knew it. But he looked at her quizzically, as though wondering why she was making such an issue out of something he thought unimportant. The Acetan liked contrasting colors; the more they clashed the more he liked them.

Aleria just stood there, her arms folded in a posture of impatience, waiting.

"I might not get it right," Jemall warned her.

"Keep trying." There was no mistaking the command in her voice. She wanted Jemall to know that she was prepared to wait forever until he produced the belt she wanted. Aleria seldom exercised her authority so vehemently, but it had suddenly occurred to her that all three of her companions were becoming just a bit too familiar. It was time to put them in their place. "Keep trying," she repeated, "until you get it right."

Jemall tried—and got it wrong. The beads changed from gold to lead to copper, from copper to oxydized bronze. Next they were rust-encrusted iron, then lead, and at last, a very tarnished silver. Trying to get them shiny, he transmuted them first to nickel, then to chrome.

"Aleria, this just isn't going to work," the bailiff protested. "Won't the chrome do?"

Aleria sighed. She'd proved her point; there was no use in overdoing it. "I guess it'll have to."

She picked up the heavy belt, strapped it around her waist, and advanced toward the deeper waters.

"All right, boys," she told them. "Let's do it."

The Acetan, the Kahikan, and the dolphin all followed at a respectful distance. Aleria in an imperious mood was not one to be trifled with.

# Chapter VII

Aleria's mood switched from imperious annoyance to enthralled fascination as they began their tour of the pellucid Kahikan waters. A chance to abandon the limited resources of Rix for anyplace else would have been sufficient to dissolve her boredom and the irritability that had resulted from it. But the underwater world through which they now voyaged afforded more than just a change of scenery; it was an opportunity to travel through a fantasy landscape beyond the imaginings of even such creative minds as those of the legendary Verne, Carroll, Baum, and even Disney.

Any ocean presented an alternative world where the laws of lands simply did not apply. Even on Earth, an undersea excursion brought one into contact with such impossible creatures as the argonaut, or paper nautilus, which took its offspring for a sail on the surface by using its fragile shell to catch the wind, or the narwhal, unicorn of the seas, which lived by spearing flatfish from the ocean floor and letting its forward thrust through the water force them to whirl down its spiral horn to its mouth. Even those same flatfish, with both eyes on the top of their heads, were strange, almost impossible creatures, as was that quick-change artist, the squid, whose chromatophores allowed it to vary the color of its body in as little as a third of a second.

Here on Kahiko, the phantasmagoria caused the wonders of Earth's waters to pale by comparison. To begin with, there was the underwater landscape itself, the hills and valleys of the ocean floor, which varied from sandy plain to muddy flat to outcroppings of bare, shale-like layers of rock. And there were pebbles, stones, and rocks of every sort imaginable, though the most frequently occurring were the type that Rosmer and Nehinei had brought back to Rix for Jemall to transmute into Aleria's weight belt. These lay scattered in quantity across the ocean floor and stood in heaps and stacks, piled upon each other in petrified groupings of every sort. Aleria wondered if perhaps great parts of the ocean floor had broken loose from those knobby outcroppings. Perhaps they were the basic stuff of the planet itself.

She had never seen rock formations like those odd mounds, and yet they reminded her of something. Jemall would know. His talent for psionic matter transmutation was based, in part, on a strange Acetan ability to "read" the atomic structure of things. She reached out and touched her bailiff's arm to get his attention.

"What—?" she began, but her voice was lost in a cascade of bubbles. You couldn't carry on a conversation under water using your voice. *What are those things?* she narrowcast at him.

Jemall tried to reply, but his voice, too, was lost in a garble of bubbles. He could only gesture helplessly, for the Acetan was a telepathic mute. He could receive her questions, but he couldn't answer them.

Reluctantly—for she disliked using it—Aleria opened her transponder channel to the ship, activating it by using the special ring she always wore. She ordered Houston to connect her with Jemall, even though that meant a three-way link, always confusing to deal with.

*You were saying?* she asked the bailiff.

*Coprolites*, he replied.

Aleria looked down at her belt in disgust. *Shit*, she muttered.

*Aw, come on*, Jemall cajoled. *It hasn't been shit in a million years. And anyway, it's been transmuted.*

*Still, it was shit once.*

*So, probably, was everything else in the universe at one time or another*, Jemall told her placatingly.

*What are you two talking about?* Rosmer wanted to know. *I can only follow one side of the conversation.*

*Those rocks*, Aleria replied with a shudder.

*The round ones?*

*Yes. They're petrified turds.*

*They're what?*

*You heard me*, Aleria told him. *Fossilized feces.*

The dolphin began to make choking noises. *Oh, and I picked one up in my mouth. Yuccchh. Gag me with a prune!*

Aleria and the others stared at him, puzzled. *What's that supposed to mean?* the judge finally asked him. *I mean, I can understand your sentiments, but that's the strangest way I've ever heard of expressing them.*

Rosmer shrugged. *It's an age-old Pacific dolphin expression. Like "fashoor."*

*What does that mean?* Aleria asked on behalf of the ship and the bailiff, who couldn't be heard by anyone but her.

*Why, it's an affirmative, the strongest one dolphins have—at least, Pacific dolphins. Atlantic dolphins tend to favor the use of "kwait," while Mediterranean dolphins tend to say "maywee." A dolphin can tell where another dolphin comes from by the expressions it uses.*

*Interesting*, said Aleria. *Fashoor. Well,* she reassured Rosmer, *Jemall says those turds have been rock for so long that they've forgotten they ever were anything else, and so can we.*

Rosmer made a wry face. *Easier said than done.* He made a series of quick dives with his mouth open, as though to rinse it out. *Well,* he said when he returned, *I guess there's nothing much I can do about it now.*

*That's right,* Aleria told him.

They had been swimming along as they spoke, and had arrived at a vast forest of tall sea grasses, pink ones and green ones, translucent all, which shimmered as they waved back and forth in the varied currents.

*How lovely!* Aleria exclaimed, and dived toward the grass forest.

Nehinei instantly interposed himself between the flame-haired judge and the enchanting seaweed. *Keep away from stands of oki,* he advised sharply.

*Why?* she asked. *It looks innocent enough. And it's beautiful!*

*Look again,* he commanded.

She did, and saw that among the waving tendrils were others, almost identical in hue and translucence, which did not appear to be attached to the bed of the sea but floated free among the sinuously-moving seaweed.

*What are those?* she asked.

*Oki fenoki,* Nehinei replied. *They fasten onto living creatures, send tendrils thorugh their victims' bloodstreams, and suck their vital juices out. They eat a fish from within, then abandon its empty shell.*

Aleria shuddered. *How awful! But how does one avoid them?*

*They never leave the oki forests except when attached to a living creature. When their host dies, they die, too; they're that deeply attached. But just before dying, they spawn.* When Aleria looked alarmed, he added, *Their larvae are harmless. They don't become dangerous until they have been fed and nurtured in the oki stands.*

*The lesson,* Jemall said through the transponder, *seems to be to avoid oki forests.*

Aleria agreed, and rapidly put a considerable distance between herself and this one. She floated along through the limpid waters, watching the various creatures scuttle along the sea bed—transparent crabs, billowing rayfish, odd little tentacled creatures that carried shells four to five times their size. (The water made such feats possible; living in the sea was not all that different from living in the weightlessness of the interstellar void, she reminded herself.)

They came at last to a vast coral city where thousands of Kahikans lived. Its many-tiered apartments had been carved from the living rock. Most of the coral in this metropolis was of the pink or red variety. With the brilliant red of the resident Kahikans' costumes, the entire area seemed to glow as though lit by a flaming sunset. Aleria was now even more grateful that Jemall had removed the pink tint from her extra eyelids; looking at a place like this through rose-colored glasses would have been overpowering.

*Talk about seeing red!* Jemall muttered through the transponder link.

*Kahikans do tend to lean toward that color,* Aleria noted. She watched the natives drifting by in pairs, in family groups, in schools like fish. One school was literally that; led by an older Kahikan, who was obviously their instructor, was a horde of naked Kahikan children. The children caused Aleria to do a double take. Either they were all girls, or—She looked more closely. She'd been right; there was a distinct absence of male genitalia.

This made her curious about the adult Kahikans. She began to watch more closely as they swam around her. In their skimpy robes, every kick that thrust them forward revealed those areas that other civilizations regarded as *private* parts. She was disappointed to discover that her surmise had been correct: none of the Kahikans appeared equipped with a male reproductive organ.

Not even Nehinei. She dropped back and watched him as he swam on ahead. Sure enough, he, too, was as undecorated between the legs as the kendolls of Earth's early atomic period. She grimaced; she had been looking forward to taking him up on his tentative advances. Now she would just have to make do with Jemall. Not that Jemall was in any way unsatisfactory, of course. Quite the contrary. It was just that Aleria liked a little variety now and then.

She was trying to overcome her disappointment when their party arrived at the center of the city. There, on a high mound that reached to within meters of the surface, stood a colonnaded temple, carved of white coral, with an open area in the center of its roof.

*You sought a place to render judgement*, Nehinei told her. *Here is the hall in which our kings are crowned, the place of important ceremonies and of the settlement of disputes.*

Aleria looked at the carved coral edifice. It was attractive, but not imposing. It was a square building, perhaps four meters on each side. Slender columns marked the four corners and supported the elaborately-carved cross beams at one-meter intervals. There appeared to be neither front nor back to the structure; it overlooked the vast crimson city in all directions from its height on the mound. Its only unusual feature was the sunlight that diffused through the thin layer of water and then streamed through the opening in the center of the roof, forming a kind of spotlight in the middle of the square of columns.

*Where do the people gather?* Aleria asked Nehinei.

*They swim wherever they choose around this structure,* he replied. *We reach our entire world at one time with our telepathy. Being here is only ceremonial. The sender stands at the center of the temple, but he could send from anywhere on Kahiko just as easily.*

Aleria nodded, understanding. *Then are there no private hearing rooms for matters that are best not made public?* she asked.

*There is one—though it is seldom used,* the Kahikan replied.

*Where is it?* Aleria inquired. She was used to holding court in courtrooms or chambers, not in the open air—or water, as the case might be.

*It is here, right beneath us.* He led her to the white coral structure. Sure enough, right in the center of its floor was another opening. This appeared to lead to a vast cave that lay beneath the great rounded hill on which the temple stood.

*Come,* invited Nehinei, holding out his hand.

*I think I'll stay out here,* said the dolphin. *I need to surface periodically for air. Caves make me claustrophobic.*

*All right,* replied Aleria. *Jemall can wait with you. We'll just be a moment.*

Jemall wasn't sure about that. *Don't you want me to come along?* he asked through the transponder.

*Sure I do,* Aleria reassured him. *But I don't want Rosmer to disappear again. Stay with him.* When Jemall still hesitated, she transmitted, *Take a good look at the Kahikan "equipment." Nothing's going to happen.* And she flashed him a mental image of what she'd noticed before.

Jemall shrugged. *All right. I guess you're right.*

*Come,* urged Nehinei again. It was clear that his invitation was meant for Aleria.

*I'd like to.* She smiled and followed him through the opening into the underwater cave.

The hearing room was as old as civilization on Kahiko. It stretched out across the golden sand of the ocean floor to great curving walls of porous gray rock that arched upward to form a dome. In the very center of the dome was the opening into the temple floor.

The great room was softly lit by distant sunlight, filtered through many meters of water. Focused by the temple's open roof and the hole in its floor, the light fell on the center of the cave in a pale shaft. The porous gray rock that made up the walls and roof of the dome was dotted here and there with what appeared to be luminous barnacles, which imparted a gentle glow to even the farthest reaches of the chamber.

*This is our seat of highest authority.* Nehinei's voice seemed to hum inside Aleria's head. *Here, from oldest times, matters of greatest gravity concerning all the denizens of Kahiko's deeps have been decided.*

He gestured toward the center of the dome, which was not only illuminated by the shaft of light from above, but which was also ringed by slender columns of white coral. Great gnarled columns of colored coral, their colors graduating from pale shell pink to a crimson that rivaled the Kahikan costumes, formed widely spaced concentric rings around the central white one.

*Our eligibility to join the Confederation is surely as important as any ruling ever made here. I trust you will find us worthy.* He smiled, then, and Aleria suddenly realized that she was not only hearing his voice humming inside her head but was also feeling its vibrations all over her body. The cavern itself had begun to vibrate with the subtle sound. Was the humming Nehinei's doing, then, or did it have something to do with this room, which seemed to have a life force of its own?

The strange chord seemed to catch at the very essence of Aleria's being. Even her bones seemed to vibrate with it—all the small, fine bones of her body, particularly those in the backs of her hands, in the front of her ears, and in her nose. It was an irresistible sensation, and Aleria found herself entranced by it.

The gentle droning continued, and at last Aleria realized that its source was indeed Nehinei, who had taken advantage of the structure of the hearing room to enhance the sound until it seemed to surround her, to bore through her, as gentle and seductive and insidious as any sound she had ever heard.

And when she glanced at him, floating just in front of her with his red netting billowing about him, she realized that male Kahikans were not, in fact, devoid of genitals; they merely stored them within their bodies, as did Earth's whales, until the need for them arose. No wonder they had thought Jemall, with his organs constantly on exhibit outside his body, the Kahikan equivalent of Priapus!

But now, as the room seemed to fill with the buzzing of a thousand bees, this humming was turning on the Kahikan as well as his guest. Nehinei's organ emerged—and what a wondrous protuberance it was; subtle and prehensile, it advanced toward her sinuously, like a tentacle, but a tentacle that appeared able to lengthen and contract itself at will.

And then Nehinei was beside her, his smooth skin pressing against the length of her body, his sinuous fingers seeming to caress every inch of her flesh at the same time. The humming sound grew louder, reverberating inside her head, inside her very soul, and somehow their garments— her silvery bikini, his red netting toga—were floating free beside them in the underwater cave. Only her weight belt remained in place, to keep her where she wanted to be, there in the center of that throbbing, vibrating cavern, with her throbbing, vibrating Kahikan lover.

Aleria discovered then that her new gill slits were the most erogenous of erogenous zones. When Nehinei ran his lips along their edges, her bones dissolved, and all her will turned to jelly. She was helpless in his hands, helpless to do anything but reach out blindly toward the source of all that pleasure, to stroke him and caress him and mirror his motions with her own. She ran her own lips and tongue along his gill slits, feeling his tongue on her gills, on her throat, in her ear, and all the while the waters were lapping, lapping against her, and the room was humming with the chord of their lovemaking.

Only then did he advance with one motion that she could not mirror, the sensuous exploration of that sensitive area between her thighs with his sinuous, prehensile organ. It searched, massaged, stimulated, wormed its way subtly in and out of her, and all she could do was let her legs float upward along his muscled flanks to encircle his waist, to allow him to obtain the maximum possible penetration.

It seemed to her as though her entire being were full of him—every cavity, every orifice—and still she couldn't get enough. She climaxed again and again, over and over, his subtle thrusting keeping her at the peak of excitement, regenerating sensation every time it began to subside.

How long they coupled like that she did not know, but, when at last Nehinei stopped, slowly letting his organ slip from her to disappear inside his own body until the next time—until the *next* time!—she felt a strange primeval sadness such as she had never known before at the end of a tryst, and, at the same time, a deeper satisfaction than she had ever experienced. She knew then that Nehinei had succeeded in what she now realized had been his goal: he had bribed the judge, and she had not only taken the bribe, but would do so again and again. She wanted more—so much more that she knew already what her decision would be: even if they were guilty of the most heinous crimes, the Kahikans would be admitted to the Confederation!

*Let me show you the other wonders of my planet*, Nehinei cajoled.

The two of them had emerged into the fading light to rejoin Rosmer and Jemall. Now Nehinei, bearing Houston's flashlight like a beacon before him, led them off across the underwater city.

Jemall was trying to get Aleria's attention. She realized that, having broken the transponder circuit when she entered the cave, she had left him mute, and she was still out of direct communication with him—something that was more of a problem for the bailiff, on this telepathic world, than it was for her. She reestablished contact with him once again, via the ship.

*What took you so long?* the bailiff demanded.

*I was inspecting the chambers.*

*And the chamberlain?*

*That is not your concern*, Aleria told him flatly. *Anyway, I have a certain tradition to maintain regarding the various chambers in which I hold court.*

*I thought that was* our *tradition*, the bailiff complained—rather petulantly, Aleria thought.

*It was* my *tradition before I ever set eyes or hands on you*, she informed him.

*With Judge Ashippun?* he gasped, astounded.

*Don't be silly. Of course not. But there was always someone around. I trust that there always will be.*

The big silver Acetan nodded. He had no strings on Aleria, nor she on him, though they enjoyed each other's company to a far greater extent than most judges and bailiffs. But Aleria knew that Jemall had a tendency to become just a little bit possessive; she found that he often had to be reminded that being her bailiff and her most frequent lover did not give him any exlusive rights.

The two of them had been glaring at each other during this exchange and had not been looking where they were going. They suddenly found themselves in the midst of a school of small golden fish. The psychic din, as all the little fish babbled nonsense at one another, was tremendous. Aleria put her hands over her ears, realized that that wouldn't block out psychic noise, and then struck out toward Nehinei with powerful strokes and even more powerful kicks. Jemall followed, and soon the two of them had outdistanced the fish.

When they caught up with Rosmer and Nehinei, Aleria commented offhandedly, *Those little yellow fish sure were noisy.*

*I could have told you that. They're just like the carp and the koi back on Earth,* Rosmer grunted. *Noisiest fish in existence—and they never have a damned thing to say.*

*You're right,* Aleria said. *You could have warned me. I had no idea that schools of fish could be so irritating.*

*Look, I can't tell you about everything in my experience. You wouldn't be able to process it fast enough. I taught you how to augment—*

*That was your job!*

*And how to screen—*

*For which I'm grateful.*

*But even if I had managed to meld with you somehow and give you the sum total of my experience, you wouldn't understand when to apply those experiences!*

*You could have given me the chance to try,* Aleria told him.

*Even if I did, half of what I know about operating under water wouldn't apply here on Kahiko. Take these oki weeds for example.*

Aleria hadn't realized that, as they argued, she and Rosmer had been drifting very near to one of the stands of oki. As a mild current eddied around them, some of the fronds seemed almost to reach out toward them. Aleria and Rosmer sidestepped, not noticing a small, separate outgrowth in the direction toward which they now swam.

*Watch out!* Jemall yelled in alarm, coming up behind them.

Aleria heard him, of course, because he'd yelled at her through the transponder. She began to backpaddle at once. But Rosmer, not being plugged in to Houston, did not, could not hear that warning shout. Jemall's mental voice was electronically created and could not be read through normal telepathic channels.

One of the free-floating tendrils of oki fenoki suddenly

shot from the edge of the oki forest and attached itself to Rosmer. The dolphin screamed, a long and terrible scream, and Aleria and Jemall pulled him from the forest's edge and began to try to pry the fenoki loose. They couldn't do it.

The dolphin continued to scream—great, anguished utterances of pain and terror. Aleria pulled her laser pistol from her belt.

*Hold still, dammit*, she cried to the writhing Rosmer, but he was too terrified to listen.

Jemall pulled loose one of his swords and sliced the body of the fenoki off as close to Rosmer's side as he could manage. Pale greenish blood surged from the open wound at the back of the fenoki's head—but the head kept its position and the teeth their grip on the terrified dolphin.

*Beheading it won't do any good*, Nehinei said, swimming up beside them, though he, too, now held one of his quartz knives in his hand. *The fenoki has fantastic regenerative powers. It can grow a whole new body from any of its twenty-seven eyes. The trick is, somehow, to blind it.* He replaced the knife in the netting of his crimson garment and took up his flashlight, shining it at full power as close as possible to the head that remained attached to Rosmer's smooth side. Aleria could see the twenty-seven blue eyes blinking in response to the unaccustomed brightness. She saw that at least one of those eyes had already begun to swell, for the purpose, she was sure, of regenerating the body of the beast.

*The light doesn't seem to be enough*, she observed. *Jemall, Nehinei—hold Rosmer steady and let me try.*

When the others had a good grip on their companion and were holding him still, Aleria reset her laser pistol to its narrowest possible beam and began to sear the head of the fenoki off Rosmer's side. A moment later, there was nothing left but a circular bite mark on the dolphin's silky flesh.

*There*, said the judge. The others relinquished their hold on the dolphin.

Rosmer took just a moment to catch his breath. *What if a tendril already got inside me?* he demanded. *It could grow and grow, and it would take over. It would eat me from the inside. I'll die!*

*No you won't*, Aleria soothed, stroking him gently down the length of his flank to calm him. *Jemall*, she said, turning to the bailiff, *can you read his cells for alien matter?*

*I can try to*, the bailiff replied. He flexed his long, four-jointed fingers in front of him, then placed the backs of his hands against his forehead and began to move his head to and fro along the length and breadth of the dolphin.

*All clear as far as I can tell*, Jemall reassured both the judge and Rosmer. *I think you can relax.*

*Maybe its blood or its germs got into my bloodstream. Are you sure it won't be able to regenerate from that?* The dolphin was still very frightened, but he seemed to have calmed down tremendously since Jemall had done his equivalent of X-raying him.

*Impossible*, Nehinei told him. *They can regenerate from their eyes, but the eyes need something to nourish them. So even if an eye got loose in your bloodstream, it couldn't regenerate, since it would be detached from the head. Relax. I've never seen as thorough a job of excising a fenoki as Aleria just did. That was fire you were using, wasn't it?*

*Yes*, Aleria told him, *one form of it*.

*Fire is even better than glass. It will save many children, many pets. When we are in the Confederation, that is what we will trade for!*

*What do you have to trade?* Aleria asked, curious. She chose to ignore the fact that he considered admission to the Confederation a foregone conclusion.

*The traders who came before seemed to like our clothing*, Nehinei told her. *We can trade our krasnicloth.*

*Is that what you call it?* Aleria asked. *It's beautiful. I was thinking, when I first saw it, that I would like a set of judicial robes made of it.*

*I thought you never wore red*, Jemall muttered. Aleria ignored him.

*I will give you such robes*, Nehinei said. *In appreciation.*

*Appreciation for what?* Jemall growled darkly through the transponder.

*I believe he is anticipating that my ruling will be in Kahiko's favor—but we can't have it look as though he were bribing the judge.*

Suddenly understanding the mental image Aleria shot him regarding the consequences of bribing a judge, Nehinei, who caught on quickly, corrected himself as tactfully as possible. *You may have robes in exchange for this coolfire-within-glass given to me by golden Houston.*

*Wonderful!* Aleria cried delightedly.

*What about me?* Jemall asked petulantly.

The Kahikan couldn't have heard him, but told him generously, *You may have robes, too.*

Jemall flashed him a brilliant smile, but Aleria snapped at Nehinei, *Bailiffs do not wear robes.*

*What do they wear?* the Kahikan asked innocently.

*Actually*, Aleria told him, *They wear whatever they please, so long as it doesn't detract from the dignity of the court.* She flashed him a series of mental pictures of some of the costumes in which Jemall had decked himself on various planets—chartreuse medieval armor, a Napoleonic uniform with a big silver codpiece, an orange thermal duck-hunting suit, even, once, a pair of magenta wading boots over a lavender jumpsuit. One of her favorites was a strange costume, indeed: he had chosen to wear a sleeveless vest over his bare chest, and, on his usually hairless head had created a sheaf of stiff straight hair, right down the middle. Feathers hung suspended from this strip of hair. For some reason, this made Jemall look particularly fearsome, as he stood, arms folded, in the front of her courtroom.

*So you see, anything goes,* she finished, *though it may seem odd garb for the courtroom. But even there he gets away with a lot, because no one knows what a bailiff from off-planet should look like.*

*I'd really like something out of that red netting,* Jemall said wistfully. *How it's cut doesn't really matter.* Aleria passed his words on.

*Leave it to me,* said their host. *It'll be perfect!*

*What're those garments made of, anyway?* Rosmer asked, much calmer now than he'd been just moments before.

*Seaweed,* Nehinei replied.

*How do you get it so red?*

*The yariika produce the dye,* Nehinei told them, flashing them all a mental image of a small, squidlike creature. *We are not far from a rakun, or yariika farm. Would you like to see it?*

Aleria, Jemall, and Rosmer responded enthusiastically to this invitation, so Nehinei made a sharp turn and led them through a pale gold sargasso grove to the well-ordered rakun. The demonstration of how the squid farmers harvested their ink was interesting, but Aleria found her thoughts wandering, returning again and again to her afternoon adventure. She had caught a subtle tone of promise in Nehinei's offer to show them the rakun. She had a feeling she was going to get to see more than just squid—and she hoped she was right. She also hoped that the wonders awaiting her were of the sort she had already been introduced to in that great cave beneath the dome of rock.

# Chapter VIII

With a certain sense of relief Aleria discovered that there was indeed some sort of industry here on Kahiko. The existence of the Kahikans had seemed too idyllic. They swam, they slept, they coupled (or tripled, or more, as the spirit moved them), they ate their meals—usually krill, or the transparent phantom shrimp that lived among the coral bases, or, on occasion, a small fish or two. But they didn't seem to work.

They didn't really have to. The waters provided all their needs, and, having no fire, they had little industry. Still, there were some who worked: the quartz shapers, who carefully chipped the stone knives that each adult Kahikan wore; the telepathic broadcasters; and the coral carvers who hewed the hollow chambers in which the Kahikans lived from the calcareous reefs and atolls. Kahikans did not choose the sites of their cities; the coelenterate polyps did that by creating the coral beds. Kahikans tended, more than any society Aleria had ever encountered, to go with the flow—in this case, the ebb and flow of the tides and the ocean currents.

Somehow, such an idyllic existence went against the grain of Aleria's very being. Raised in an industrial society—even though it was a highly automated one—she had always believed that you justified your existence by the work that you did. While she conceded that the Kahikans were beautiful, she could not quite accept the idea that beauty was its own excuse for being, that form without function did not have to be rationalized. Seeing the squid farming operation made it easier for her to accept this society.

The rakun were run rather on the order of dairy farms back on Earth. The squid were allowed to graze in the krill fields but were herded into the carved-coral barns at half-day intervals so that the Kahikans could collect their ink. The only real difference was that, on Earth, dairy cattle were kept as calm as possible, whereas the squid were agitated at milking time to make them release their dye. Watching the milking process, Aleria began to pick up vibrations of discomfort. She glanced toward Rosmer and saw that he was feeling the same thing.

As unobtrusively as possible, she inched toward the dolphin and narrowcast her intent to augment his reception. He nodded imperceptibly, and Aleria shut off the transponder connection that linked her with the ship and the bailiff. She would need all of her powers of concentration for the task at hand.

The augmentation revealed that the squid were, indeed, somewhat intelligent—about as intelligent as domestic cattle on earth, but not as intelligent as those bovines that still roamed free in wildlife preserves, in herds as ancient as time itself. Aleria was not sure whether she was disappointed at this finding or relieved. The squid obviously had not sent the mysterious appeal. In fact, they were rather silly animals, almost as silly as sheep. They had indeed been protesting the ink harvest—but, for the most part, only because they were unhappy with their neighbors at the inking machines. The yariika were not the source of the message that had brought her here.

Who was? Aleria had no idea. Neither did Rosmer. Realizing that their investigation was not to be ended so easily, Aleria cajoled Nehinei into showing her more of the rakun. He was more than happy to do so and proudly introduced her to its frolicking, whiplike electric eels. They performed a function not unlike that of sheepdogs, protecting and corraling the yariika as they grazed. Like sheepdogs, the eels were friendly and fairly intelligent— just about as intelligent as dogs, when you got right down to it—but they were not the source of that desperate cry for help. They appeared to be quite content with their lot, and they were certainly in no danger of extinction, though they had been somewhat inbred to bring out traits like swiftness and strength of electric shock. This wasn't a judge's concern; the selective breeding of lower animals had never been considered worthy of interplanetary intervention. Besides, the eels didn't seem upset by it.

The krill, too, seemed to accept their lot. They had been the natural food of squid since time immemorial; they were not intelligent enough to worry about it.

Who had sent that message, Aleria wondered, *who?* But there was no ready answer. And despite the conductivity of the water, she had picked up no further signals since submerging herself. She would have to try another approach.

*Do you have any other domesticated animals?* Aleria asked Nehinei, hoping this might give her a lead. *Any zoos, perhaps?*

*What's a zoo?* he asked her, and she flashed him a mental image of some of her favorite zoological parks on Earth and other planets.

*They're kept in cages?* Nehinei gasped, astonished. *That's barbaric!*

*Sometimes it's done for their own protection,* Aleria protested, but to someone who had never known animals to be imprisoned, she had to concede that zoos were a barbaric notion. She wasn't used to having to apologize for the civilization from which she'd come; she didn't like the feeling it gave her at all.

*We don't have anything like that on Kahiko,* Nehinei told her, *but we do keep pets. They stay with us as long as they want to, then move on.*

*Like cats,* Aleria mused.

*What's a cat?*

Aleria showed him by mental picture.

*An interesting creature,* Nehinei said thoughtfully, *but I'm not at all sure I'd like to meet one. You say they eat fish?*

Aleria nodded.

*I suppose they don't distinguish between intelligent fish and dumb animals?*

Aleria laughed. *There was a time when cats were considered "dumb animals." In fact, there was a time when the men of Earth slaughtered whales and dolphins for the oil in their bodies, not realizing they were sentient.*

*How awful,* Nehinei gasped, and Aleria could tell that he was genuinely shocked. This made her doubly dubious that the Kahikans were slaughtering an intelligent race. Either Nehinei was the most accomplished actor she had ever met, or he was truly sincere, and the dolphins' interpretation of the message had been in error. Dolphins were after all, due to their history, greatly sensitive to threats of slaughter.

*We don't hold it against man anymore*, Rosmer interjected. *Men claim to have reformed. But, of course, we tend to keep them at a safe distance whenever they go into their periodic rages. At one time they nearly destroyed our home planet with atomic devices. The Orono do not believe man has truly outgrown that phase.*

Aleria had begun to chafe at Rosmer's denunciation of the human race until it occurred to her that, like her, he was fishing for information. But either the Kahikans were truly innocent or Nehinei refused to take the bait. He clicked his tongue in sympathy and discreetly changed the subject, as would any good host.

*I keep pets*, he said brightly. *Kolenya. Would you like to see them?*

*Sure*, Aleria replied, but Rosmer was becoming bored.

*Mind if I just have a general look around the farm?* he asked.

Nehinei shrugged. *Whatever turns you on.*

Aleria looked at him sharply. Was there a hidden meaning in the way he used that phrase?

Jemall, who had been trailing along behind them, listening to their conversation but unable to contribute to it, now touched Aleria on the shoulder to get her attention. She reconnected her link to him, via Houston.

*Yes, boys?* she asked them both.

*Nothing going on up here*, said the ship.

*Nothing going on down here, either*, the bailiff complained. *Look, Aleria, how about if I hang around with Rosmer? He spent a lot of time down here before that authorization came through. I'll bet he knows where the action is.*

Aleria had the feeling that she was going to see a lot more action with Nehinei than Rosmer and Jemall could uncover, but she wasn't sure that her Kahikan guide was into group gropes, and she certainly wasn't about to discourage him from repeating the activities of that afternoon. Come to think of it, Neninei alone was as effective as any group she'd ever encountered. Aleria sent Jemall off after Rosmer with her blessings. You never knew—they just might manage to uncover the source of the mysterious message that had brought them to Kahiko, and, if not, they might come up with something rather more precious than the coprolites they had brought back to Rix. Pearls, for instance; Aleria wouldn't have minded some nice pearls as a souvenir of her stay on this planet.

She smiled to herself. Of course, Nehinei himself was the real pearl. She wondered what he had up his figurative sleeve this time.

What he had were his kolenya, which turned out to be a litter of semiintelligent octopi. They were as friendly as puppies and fell over each other in bumbling eagerness when she reached out to pet them. Though she had never expected to consider an octopus cute, these were, and she told Nehinei as much.

*They're smart, too*, he said. *They can do all kinds of things.*

*Really?*

*To borrow an expression from our dolphin friend, "fashoor." In fact, the suma miners use specially trained kolenya to help gather sumati.*

Sumati—he had used that word before. "In the throes of sumati," he had said. *What's sumati?* Aleria asked. *What are suma?*

*Sumati is the most precious substance on Kahiko*, Nehinei

confided. *We get it from the great suma.* He flashed her an image of a giant clam. *I will try to obtain some for you, though it will not be easy. Sumati is very rare. It is the only reason Kahikans work, since the sea provides our other needs.*

Wondering if sumati were pearls, or some rare Kahikan version of them, Aleria bestowed her most flirtatious smile upon Nehinei and told him coyly, *I'm sure I'd like sumati!*

The Kahikan smiled back. *I'm certain of it*, he told her. *But first let me show you some of the accomplishments of my kolenya.*

He narrowcast an image to them, and the kolenya began to dance in a circle, each one chasing the trailing legs of the koleno ahead of it. Aleria laughed delightedly as the kolenya swam up above Nehinei's head and made him appear to be juggling. Then they swam over to her in the same formation, dancing about her head.

*What else can they do?* she inquired.

*Watch*, he commanded. He signaled once again, and suddenly four of the kolenya seized her by the wrists and ankles and pulled her into a coral bower that stood nearby.

*What the hell do you think you're doing?* Aleria demanded indignantly.

*Shhh*, the Kahikan told her. *Nothing I didn't do this afternoon—but in a different way. I think you'll like it.*

Aleria had her reservations. She didn't like being in any situation where she wasn't in control—at least of herself. And the kolenya were clearly in control here.

They were surprisingly strong. The four that were holding her grasped the corner pillars with some of their legs while holding her firmly with the remaining ones; she found herself spreadeagled just above the sand floor, positioned face upward so that she could see the varicolored sea anemones that formed the roof of the bower.

Nehinei loosened the strings of her silver bikini and slipped it from her, and she was helpless to resist. She also wasn't quite sure she wanted to. When he untied the silver cord that bound her abundant red-gold hair, it floated free in the gentle currents, billowing about her head like a halo. Nehinei was gentle, and she knew instinctively that this was a game, that he would never hurt her. But when she tried to free her hands and feet, the kolenya gripped her more tightly. She was totally within their power—and Nehinei's.

The Kahikan had removed his own red robe, and his strange, flexible organ had begun to emerge once more from its secret place. He advanced toward her and began to tease her every orifice with his tongue, his fingers, the cilia of his gills, and that wonderful, flexible instrument of his.

He wasn't humming this time, but Aleria's body was. Nehinei seemed to be everywhere at once, and she suddenly realized that the remaining kolenya had joined him and were caressing her sides, her back, her sensitive inner thighs, even as he made her mouth, her gills, and every other aperture hunger for this touch. Her body had developed a will of its own. Even her hair, moving in the currents caused by their conjoining, seemed sinuously alive as it wrapped around him, tickled her own body, bound them together in a red-gold tangle that obscured her vision, so that she was all skin and nerve endings and a glorious sense of touch.

It was too much. She writhed and tried to wrest herself from this sweet agony, but the kolenya held her fast, their grip at once gentle and as enduring as steel. All around her the waters were lapping, lapping at every inch of her flesh like a thousand tongues, while the kolenya tentacles and Nehinei's own tongue and his flexible organ aroused her to peaks she had never before experienced and then, when she thought no more was possible, took her ever onward, upward, higher, deeper, soaring, floating until she could bear it no longer.

The telepathic Nehinei was inside her mind as well as her body. He knew the moment she reached that highest all possible points and allowed her to climax while sharing with her his own sensations at that moment. In mental contact with him, experiencing his ecstasy as well as her own, she felt her body and her mind explode with rapture, filling her, filling him, floating within and without her own being, free as the fanning fenoki, yet fastened securely to the brilliant bower by the powerful grip of the kolenya. Then, drifting in the calm of the quiet sea, she slept.

When she awoke, the kolenya were gone. She floated in Nehinei's arms within the coral bower. He brushed her hair away from her face and smiled at her, and she smiled back.

*That was wonderful*, she told him. *But I think we should get back to the others now, though I really haven't the strength.*

*I have seen to it that they are occupied for the evening*, Nehinei informed her. *Spend the night here in my arms. Tomorrow we will continue our tour of Kahiko.*

*And you will show me more wonders?* the judge asked, amused.

*If you like. Perhaps I will even find sumati for you. The best is yet to come.*

It seemed to her that his message carried a dual meaning,

but she was too exhausted to analyze it. *You're sure that Rosmer and Jemall won't be looking for us?* she asked languidly.

*I doubt it*, replied Kahikan. *We will find them in the morning.*

*If you say so*, Aleria murmured, and was instantly asleep once more.

What Nehinei had provided for Rosmer and Jemall was half a dozen Kahikan women who had ostensibly been employed to show them the seaweed-weaving portion of the rakun operation. Fine tendrils of elastic sea vines were harvested at a specific point of porosity. The Kahikans did the harvesting themselves, since they knew of no animals—not even the kolenya—that could judge this point of ripeness accurately.

The women slipped the sea vines into great chambered shells that had been abandoned by their former inhabitants, which must have resembled the Earth creature called the chambered nautilus, Jemall guessed. Then the women filled the shells with the dye gathered from the squid and sealed them with a flat shell like Earth's sand dollar. They buried the sealed shells in the sand for three months before they removed them and began weaving the sea vines into red fabric.

Kahikan women made a special art of weaving these sea vines. Each had her own pattern, handed down in her family for generations. The results were treasured for their decorative design and for their flexibility; Kahikan netting had to expand or contract to suit its wearer's needs, and only certain kinds of knots could do that.

Having shown Jemall and Rosmer the vine-gathering, dying, and weaving operations, the six Kahikan females enticed them into a bed of sponges and seduced them repeatedly, in one innovative way after another. At first the Acetan and the dolphin were too tempted to protest, and afterward, too spent. The women aroused them over and over, again and yet again. Jemall, whose sexual energies almost never flagged, found them flagging now. Not that he wasn't enjoying himself, of course, but the Kahikan women didn't seem to know the meaning of the word "stop." It was some time before it occurred to him that, being telepathically mute, he had not been able to make his protests known to them. Not that it would have done any good if he had, for the dolphin had protested throughout—though, of course, not too strenuously—and the Kahikan women had ignored his remonstrances totally.

Jemall found the Kahikan women fascinating. They were, of course, amphibious like their males, but they did not fit the picture of mermaids according to the traditions of Earth. Jemall had always wondered how one would couple with a woman whose nether half was a fish's tail; he had said as much to Rosmer at one point when they were still aboard ship, where Jemall could speak. Rosmer had promised to complete his education for him if the opportunity ever arose. The Kahikan women were constructed—except for their gills and the positions of their heads—much like human women, and Jemall had never had difficulty in figuring out what to do with any humanoid female. That the Kahikan women regarded him as a god—and as the god of procreation—undoubtedly made his conquest easier, but, as the night wore on and the Kahikan females proved ever more insatiable, Jemall began to wonder just who had conquered whom.

And throughout these adventures he was mute, unable to protest, unable even to offer any suggestion except by gesture. Of course, he could listen to *their* conversations, except when they narrowcast intentionally in order to leave him out. This they did whenever they were plotting some new variation to try on him, something they did every time they thought his interest might be flagging. Rosmer kept up a running patter with his women through *his* adventures, enticing, teasing, cajoling—and sending them over to work on Jemall whenever the dolphin decided to take a rest.

There was no rest for the Acetan. At last, when he thought they had tried every possible variation and he was trying to catch his breath while amusedly watching the dolphin dive between the legs of their Kahikan companions, he picked up a narrowcast from his performing friend: *If you want to transmute a couple of these ladies into more traditional mermaids, I don't think they'd mind. And I can satisfy your curiosity and show you how it's done.*

Jemall nodded, and Rosmer quickly explained the process of psionic transmutation—as he understood it—to their companions. The Kahikan women were more impressed with Jemall's talents than ever before—his transmutation abilities obviously proved he was a god—and every one of them volunteered to be turned into a mermaid. Jemall was exhausted, and he wasn't sure he could get the formula straight, especially since he wasn't absolutely certain of the Kahikan molecular structure. Still, he was too tired to argue—not that he could have done so without a transponder. Besides, he was truly curious about the modus operandi one applied with mermaids. So he concentrated on the Kahikans, got as good a fix as he could on their cell structure, and mumbled a charm to himself. His mumbling sent up a cascade of bubbles from his mouth, causing the Kahikan women to giggle, but they stopped as he flexed his long, four-jointed fingers once, twice, a third time, casting his psionic spell.

The woman nearest him developed a tail all right, but it was covered with long blue-green ostrichlike feathers rather than with scales.

*Not quite*, Rosmer told him.

Jemall shrugged and flexed his fingers again. The next woman got a fish tail, but also kept her legs.

*Nope*, Rosmer said.

Jemall wanted to protest, but he knew no one could hear him. The two women were considering their new nether parts with curious amusement.

Rosmer flashed Jemall a picture of what the construction was supposed to look like. The bailiff held on to this image, concentrating with all his might, and got it right with the next female. When the dolphin voiced his approval, Jemall hastily converted the remaining three females to mermaids of Earth tradition. Then he returned the first two to their original form—something he was almost reluctant to do because he found feathers, soggy though they were becoming, rather attractive—and managed to make them match the others.

The bailiff nodded to the dolphin, as though to say, *All right, your move, friend.* And the dolphin took him up on the offer. He began a flirtatious mating dance with the nearest female, ultimately coaxing her into the proper attitude, then penetrating her with his os penis.

*So that's how it's done!* Jemall thought. One of the great mysteries of the Earth had been solved, like the puzzle of what a Scot wore under his kilt, or the dilemma of what container to keep a universal solvent in. *Well, nothing ventured, nothing gained*, the Acetan chided himself and, following Rosmer's lead, took on the next Kahikan female.

He came to the conclusion that mermaids were not all they'd been cracked up to be. They had fins in the most inappropriate places, their scales were scratchy, and their lack of legs made it too easy to become separated from one's partner in peaks of passion. Those were the times when the agile Aleria usually gripped his torso with her thighs or locked her ankles around his neck. The mermaids could not manipulate their tails in such practical ways, and Jemall found himself constantly slipping out of the appropriate orifice.

By the time he and Rosmer had finished with the first two Kahikan females, the bailiff had come to the conclusion that Rosmer might be better designed for the lower quarters and he for the top. He tried to convey this by gesture to the dolphin, who didn't quite understand him. He tried again, and this time he managed to get through. The third female was serviced by both of them at the same time. She seemed to enjoy it; Rosmer and Jemall certainly did.

But when they approached the fourth, the fifth and sixth joined in. Thus, while the Acetan made love to the top half of one mermaid, and the dolphin to her nether regions, a second Kahikan mermaid engaged the parts of Jemall's body not otherwise occupied, while a third managed to titillate the more sensitive portions of the dolphin's anatomy. The three mermaids who had already taken their turns cheered the others on with an eerie sound that reminded Jemall of nothing so much as the droning of bees of a lazy summer afternoon—or perhaps, a distant motor at the far end of languid lake.

The droning became louder, reverberating inside Jemall's

head, echoing inside the dolphin's, and Jemall, usually psychically immune, became one with Rosmer and all of the women. The humming filled his head, his soul, building to a crescendo, and he and the dolphin and the six Kahikan mermaids became a slithering, silky tangle, like silvery minnows in a net, above, around, over and inside each other, smooth and slippery, sliding and gripping, soaring and humming, humming, humming. Buzzing like all the bees in the galaxy, the water world of Kahiko seemed to explode with their pleasure, and the last thought Jemall had before drifting off to a well-earned rest was that this must have been what Homer meant by the siren song, these must have been what he had in mind when he spoke of the sirens themselves.

# Chapter IX

"What was—?" Levis Ostego began, then stopped himself. He glanced at his supervisor and saw that Medina had frozen right in the middle of scanning a readout, and was sitting at her monitor, staring into space in a kind of trance. Her face seemed oddly flushed. "Medina?" Levis asked.

She looked up, startled, then shook her head rapidly, several times, as though to clear it. "Mermaids," she muttered.

Levis sighed with relief. "You felt it, too. What a relief! I thought I'd suddenly started having hallucinations. But what—?"

Medina pursed her lips, thinking. "I wonder if it has anything to do with the Ring."

"What do you mean?"

"Well, we *have* been practicing augmenting with them. And *they're* tuned into Rosmer. Maybe we were picking up on something he was sending them."

Levis chuckled, then shook his head. "That did not

seem to be the kind of thing one would intentionally send across the interstellar void. It was too"—he searched for the right word—"personal, wouldn't you say?"

Medina smiled rather ruefully and rubbed her neck where gill slits would have been had she possessed them. "I know what you mean. Still, we don't really know our dolphin friends all that well. Maybe members of a Ring would want to share things like that with one another."

"Do you really think that was a communication—an intentional communication?"

Medina shrugged. "I don't know. I only know that it was a very powerful image and one I'm not likely to forget for quite a while."

Levis nodded. "Me, too."

The two of them sat there quietly for a moment, lost in thought. Then Medina opened the intercom to Jedrek Kabeel, her supervisor. "Levis and I have to check something out with the dolphins. Can you cover us for a few minutes?"

"I can, but I'd like to know why. This has been happening altogether too often of late."

"Jedrek, I told you we're on the verge of a real breakthrough in interstellar communications. We think—well, something just happened that we have to check with them about."

"If it came through on the monitors, shouldn't I be in on it, too?" Kabeel growled.

"It wouldn't make any sense to you," Medina told him. "It doesn't really make any sense to us. That's why we have to get over to the dolphin tank."

"All right," Kabeel grumbled. "But there's no one else available, so I'll have to come down and cover for you. Don't make a habit of this."

"We won't," Medina assured him.

Off to one side, out of video range, Levis was smiling. He knew that Kebeel had lost his power to discipline them the moment Medina and Levis had started to agument the Ring. The supervisor could make things difficult for them, bureaucratically, but they functioned on a different level now, almost in another dimension, outside his jurisdiction and understanding. They had talents beyond his ken, and those talents—possibly unique in the Confederation service— were valuable to the service. They knew it, and Kabeel knew it too.

Levis was eager to experiment further with those newly developing talents. By the time Medina had clicked off the intercom and set the monitors, he was on his feet and halfway out the door.

"No need to rush," Medina told him, but she, too, was hurrying, and not just because she wanted to commune with the Ring once more. Levis knew that, like him, Medina had had that dream—a waking dream like none either of them had ever known in sleep or even under the influence of mind expanders. It had been more than a powerful dream; it had been a shared experience, though *whose* experience they could not tell.

The two of them were off down the curving corridors of the monitoring station as soon as their machines had registered the switchover. The dolphins would have the answer. The dolphins *had* to have the answer.

The dolphins had the answer, all right, and it distressed them greatly.

*This just doesn't happen among Orono*, Selmar fretted. *Oh, I'm so ashamed. We're all so ashamed. How will we ever be able to dive with pride among the Orono of the Earth again?*

*Fashoor*, the others agreed.

Levis and Medina had become familiar with that strange dolphin term of confirmation. But they had never seen the Ring this agitated.

"What's wrong?" Levis inquired innocently.

*Why are you here?* Selmar demanded.

Levis was taken aback. "You mean we aren't welcome? I thought—I mean, we've been augmenting. We've become so close—"

*Don't be silly. Of course you're welcome. But why are you here now?*

Levis shrugged. "We had the dream, this sensation—"

*Exactly!*

"Huh?" Levis and Medina both gaped at the fuming dolphin.

*Shut your mouths. You look like silly fish*, snapped Selmar. When they had complied, he went on, *It was no dream. Rosmer, who certainly should know better, was broadcasting. Broadcasting! If you picked up on it, don't you think the rest of the world did? The rest of the universe?*

"Kabeel didn't seem to have," Medina observed.

*Well, that's a relief*, Selmar noted sourly. *That means only sensitives like you and the entire Orono population were privy to Rosmer's waking wet dream.*

"What *are* you talking about?" Medina demanded.

*Rosmer was having himself a little—what's the legal term for it? Frolic and detour, that's it.*

"With mermaids?" Levis asked, beginning to understand.

*You've got it.*

"And trained octopi?" Medina gasped.

Levis looked at her oddly. "I don't get any vibes about trained octopi."

Medina blushed. "My sensitivity rating is higher than yours, remember?"

But Carswell, the most reticent of the Ring members, was looking at her oddly. *You picked up on the octopi, too?*

Medina nodded.

*I don't think that was part of Rosmer's experience.*

"Then whose?"

The dolphin gave the mental equivalent of a shrug. *Maybe the judge has been having herself a frolic and detour, too.*

Medina gasped again, but Selmar seemed relieved. *Maybe she's the one who isn't screening*, he said, grasping at straws. Then he did the dolphin version of shaking his head, a funny kind of side-to-side quiver. *No, she couldn't send that powerfully. It must have been Rosmer. Oh, the shame of it!*

*To the max*, Sebrook agreed.

When Medina and Levis looked puzzled, Sebrook explained that this was another Pacific Orono expression—meaning, he said, that Selmar's words didn't begin to express the degree of shame that Rosmer had brought them.

But Carswell wasn't so sure. *If three of us—and Levis and Medina—have trouble sending a narrowcast all that way, how can Rosmer, with only Judge Farrell augmenting him, broadcast like that?*

"Maybe the Acetan is augmenting, too?" Levis suggested helpfully.

The dolphins were scornful. *He's a telepathic mute. He couldn't possibly augment. He can barely* hear *a broadcast when it's right next to him.*

"But isn't he a shape-changer?" Levis persisted. "Couldn't he change himself, give himself the ability?"

Selmar looked at him in disgust. *He isn't a shape-changer. He practices psionic matter transmuation. That's just a sensitivity to the atomic structures of things. He can transmute objects into other objects, atoms into other atoms, molecules into other molecules. But he can't give those molecules life—or properties they wouldn't normally possess. If he were to create a human out of the various elements your body contains, he would have just that—a body, as dead as the carbon and calcium and selenium and iron from which he had created it—or the rocks from which he had transmuted those elements.*

"What happens if he transmutes a living person into a rock?" Medina asked, curious.

*That person would be as dead as the rock he had been transformed into.*

"Oh," said Medina. "But I thought— Don't Acetans change their own shapes?"

*From one living form to another living form,* Carswell told her.

"Then couldn't he transmute himself into a dolphin with a talent for telepathy?" Levis asked.

Carswell considered that for a moment. *I don't think so. Telepathy is a property. He can't transmute a property unless it comes with the original molecule. I doubt very much that Jemall is augmenting.*

Then Medina suddenly remembered the message Garcia had brought in from Aleria Farrell—the one that had come in the drone carrier. "The Kahikans!" she cried. "Could they—?"

She never got to finish the thought. All three dolphins seized upon it.

*Of course!*

*Fashoor!*

*I think you've found the answer, dear,* Carswell told her benignly. *They must be powerful telepaths indeed to be able to broadcast like that.*

*And very impolite ones,* Selmar added.

*Ours is not to judge the societal standards of others,* Carswell chided him gently. *Perhaps, on Kahiko, it is considered polite to share this kind of experience with the rest of the planet.*

*Then why haven't we ever picked up on something like this before?* Sebrook demanded.

*Perhaps we have, and didn't know it. We may only know it now because Rosmer and Judge Farrell are plugged in to this transmission. In effect, they're translating it for us.*

"Do you think Rosmer and Aleria know that they've been broadcasting—or *what* they've been broadcasting?" Medina asked.

*Perhaps not,* Carswell mused.

*Oh, fashoor not, or they wouldn't have done it. Rosmer would never do anything like that if he knew what was happening,* Sebrook defended the absent member of his Ring.

"And Kabeel didn't pick up on it. Maybe we're receiving it because we're plugged in to them," Levis added hopefully.

*A circumstance devoutly to be desired,* Selmar intoned.

*In any case, we ought to warn them,* Carswell declared. *If they know we can read them . . .*

Levis rolled up his sleeves in preparation for dangling his arms in the tank. He had found that physical contact with the Ring improved his connection with them.

"Let's get started," he suggested. But thinking about the waking dream he had had, he was not altogether certain he wanted broadcasts of that sort to stop. He looked up and met Medina's eyes, and realized with a jolt that his supervisor was approaching this augmentation with the same reluctance.

Aleria awoke reluctantly from a dream she didn't really want to desert, to find herself cradled in Nehinei's arms. He was gazing gently down at her, and when she looked into his eyes, she realized for the first time what an unusual color they were, a pale, pale, bluish green like the watery brilliance of an aquamarine. Almost unmarred by darker rim, they seemed to be a reflection, almost a part, of the Kahikan waters themselves.

Nehinei himself was iridescent, shimmering, aquamarine flecked with an odd combination of green and silvery mauve. He was beautiful, Aleria thought, with the strange, unearthly beauty one sometimes found on distant planets, a beauty that eluded the human race but was nevertheless fascinatingly attractive once one had shelved one's prejudices—and sometimes even when one hadn't. Like a naiad, she told herself, or a mermaid. What had brought mermaids to her mind? She had been dreaming a whale song, but fish-tailed women had been part of it, somehow, though their tails were mammalian, horizontal like the flukes of whales, rather than vertical like the tails of fish.

"Mermaids," she muttered, then realized that she was still under water, that her words had been lost in a cascade of little bubbles.

But Nehinei had picked up on the muffled sound or the impulse of her thought. *Your friends*, he told her.

*Huh?* She was still half asleep. His response made no

sense to her. It sang in her head like the grammar school maxim taught to children about police: "The mermaid is your friend."

Nehinei chuckled. *Do you want to go back to sleep? Day and night do not matter beneath our waters.*

Aleria shook her head. *I have a mission here. What about my friends?*

*Your friend who looks like a god but claims not to be has used his godlike powers to transform six chosen females into the shape of fish women. Mermaids, you call them. They rejoice in having known his ministrations in this shape.*

*How do you know that?* Aleria demanded.

*They have conveyed.*

*What?*

He flashed her a complex, wordless image that illustrated the term "conveyed" for her. The private details of their lives, which most other races kept to themselves, Kahikans shared out of social duty.

Aleria was appalled. *Does that mean that the rest of Kahiko has enjoyed our intimate moments?*

*Last night, yes—but I have saved our experience in the cave to broadcast later.*

Aleria groaned. Receiving an image conveyed by a telepath was like experiencing it yourself. That meant that the whole planet had had her at the same time Nehinei and his kolenya had.

Nehinei was alarmed at her distress. *It is not a custom among your people to share such joys with others?*

*No, it is not!* she snapped, but she stopped to consider. The makers of sexually explicit videos certainly attempted to "convey," as did the writers of similar books—but, no, those were fiction, elaborating on acts that might never have taken place. Even the authors of tell-all autobiographies told all after the fact, when the experiences had been filtered through memory. That wasn't the same as having your intimate moments shared by all the inhabitants of a planet at the exact second you experienced them yourself. Aleria felt that was somehow an invasion of privacy. She told Nehinei as much.

*Well, not to worry,* he reassured her. *We were preempted.*

She looked at him quizzically. *How?*

*Your friends and the mermaids. Their activity was much more interesting, didn't you think?*

And Aleria suddenly realized that, even as she had soared with Nehinei to new heights of passion, held in the gentle grip of his kolenya, her mind had been tickled by other images, those of a tribe of fish-tailed women who were simultaneously being serviced—by Rosmer and Jemall, she now realized; she recognized them both from the memory of the fantasy. It had been a compound projection; now she recognized the women from their cognizance of each other's presence—and from the dolphin's vision of them as well. No doubt Houston had received a mindful from Jemall, who was mute without the transponders. She was grateful to the ship for screening out *that* signal, at least.

But poor Houston! He was so prim, almost prissy in his attitudes toward sex. As a machine, he found humans' and humanoids' pleasures in the act of reproduction a totally illogical failing on their part. He would not have been happy to receive a transmission of an orgiastic experience—with mermaids, no less!—from the bailiff.

Aleria decided she'd better check in with him and calm him down if he was agitated. She took off her ring and established the transponder connection.

*About time you checked in*, Houston groused.

*Have you heard from Jemall?* the judge asked warily, prepared for a tirade.

*Not a word since yesterday*, Houston replied. *Isn't he with you?*

*Not exactly.* Aleria was relieved. At least Jemall had managed to keep his mental mouth shut, even if Rosmer hadn't. *But I know where he is*, she hastened to reassure the ship. *We're headed that way now so that we can continue our investigation.* She broke the connection.

*Well*, she told Nehinei, *let's not make a liar out of me. Let's go find the others and continue on our inspection of the planet.*

The Kahikan nodded. *What would you like to see next?*

*Your other industry. Sumati.*

*Sumati is not an industry*, he corrected her usage. *It is a product. The industry is sumati-gathering. Those who do it are an unusual bunch. It takes a strange type of Kahikan to live alone, far from any school or city, to watch the suma day and night for the exact moment to gather sumati. It takes a strong Kahikan to give up the sumati he has gathered—and, of course, the sumati-barss do not give up their sumati lightly.*

*Sumati-barss?*

*The gatherers. My brother is one. I'll take you to meet him.*

They had reached the coral corral where the dolphin, the Acetan, and the six mermaids rested after their exertion of the night before.

*All right, you guys, get with it*, Aleria ordered the dolphin and the bailiff. *We're off to see the wizard.*

*Is it morning already?* Jemall asked through the transponder.

*It sure is.*

*Let's try for afternoon*, he said, turning over and trying to go back to sleep.

*Come on*, Aleria cajoled. *Where's that famous Acetan regenerative power?*

*Regenerating*, he groaned.

Aleria chuckled. *Well, it took a water planet, but I see you're finally in over your head.*

*I don't find my present state amusing.* The Acetan stretched, then began to dive through the nearby waters in an attempt to wake himself up.

*There's a cold spring just over the rise*, Nehinei offered helpfully.

*Thanks*, said the Acetan, and headed in that direction.

Aleria turned to the dolphin. *Now you*, she ordered. *Wake up.*

*Bummer*, growled Rosmer.

*What's that supposed to mean?* the judge demanded.

*Like, barf me out. I want to bag some more zees.*

*Rosmer, wake up. Speak Standard.*

The dolphin shook himself. *Sorry.*

*What were you saying?*

*Just using some old Pacific dolphin expressions. Sorry about that, chief.*

*Don't call me chief*, Aleria muttered absently. *Just wake up and let's get going.*

*Right. Be right back as soon as I get a breath of fresh air.* The dolphin headed for the surface. Aleria watched him go, struck, as always, by the grace of his movement in the water.

Just then, Jemall returned and was greeted by a chorus of giggles from the Kahikan mermaids. They were pointing delightedly at his silvery staff, which now hung downward, and the tripartite sac that backed it up. They began to approach him.

*No way, girls*, he told them, forgetting they couldn't hear him.

But Aleria could. *Jemall, do I sense reluctance? From you?*

*That you do. Would you please tell them we've got work to do?*

Aleria chuckled. *When a Kahikan's organ leaves his body, it means that he's ready and willing to perform. Since yours is always on the outside, they figure you're signaling that you want to have another go.*

*Please explain that I do not*, the bailiff begged. *Last night was, as our dolphin friend would say, a totally awesome experience*. However, that doesn't mean I'm in a hurry to repeat it. Please tell them.

Aleria nodded and attempted to convey his message as tactfully as possible. The Kahikan women looked disappointed. But when Aleria told them that Jemall would return them to their former shapes, they grew very agitated, and protested vehemently.

*They seem to like their new look*, Aleria commented dryly. *You're off the hook, Jemall. You don't have to transmute them back this morning.*

*A good thing*, he replied. *I don't think I could possibly get it right in the state I'm in.*

Aleria had no doubt that he was correct about his diminished powers. She had seen his spells go awry in the past and had no desire to see him mess up when transmuting a living creature. For the time being, at least, she was glad the women wanted to retain their new shapes, although they couldn't do so for very long. It wasn't exactly Confederation policy to create new races on other planets, and she and Jemall would have to answer for creating mermaids on Kahiko unless they could convince the Kahikan women to allow Jemall to change them back.

But that could come later, when she had the energy for it. Rosmer returned, and Nehinei led them off on their special tour of the watery wonderland.

As daylight filtered through the waters, the rays of the Kahikan sun were almost visible in the depths. Looking up toward the surface, Aleria found a surprise: her circular view of the air above the surface of the Kahikan sea encompassed an even wider vision, but seemed to be surrounded by a reflection of the bottom. Startled, she passed the image on to Houston and asked him what it meant.

*Refraction*, he explained. *The light refracts up to an angle of forty-eight-point-eight degrees. Beyond that it reflects off the water.*

*That means I have a blind spot, doesn't it?*

*Yes. The surface beyond a ninety-seven-point-six degree angle. But what you see within that angle may lie beyond it because of refraction.*

*I'm not sure I understand*, Aleria told him.

*You probably won't be able to without years of experience*, the ship replied. *Just remember that whatever you see may be an illusion, and you'll be all right.*

*Terrific*, Aleria muttered in disgust. Well, it didn't matter that she couldn't see the whole surface all the way to the horizons; nothing much happened on the surface of Kahiko. She turned her attention back to the wondrous depths.

And the waters' depths were wondrous indeed. As their group zigged around schools of jellyfish, with their trailing, transparent tentacles, and zagged between sargasso masses and kelp clumps, she watched seeming rocks come to life, becoming great turtlelike creatures. Sea eels slithered from their lairs, sea horses galloped by, squid sailed on the currents. Flying fish gathered momentum and broke through the surface, to return to the waters at far-distant destinations. There were fish of every shape and color, and some that were nearly transparent, their pulsing veins and their bone structures visible through their translucent skins.

True fish, false fish, crustaceans, mollusks—there were sea creatures of every sort—but, Aleria realized, there were no mammals other than the amphibious humanoid Kahikans. She had dreamed a whale song, but upon waking heard none.

*Are there no other mammals on Kahiko?* she inquired of Nehinei.

*Mammals?*

She explained, adding that it was unusual that the Kahikans would be the only mammalian form to survive on the planet.

*There is another*, Nehinei told her ominously.

*There is? Are they intelligent?*

*Theirs is a feral intelligence. They are killers. They prey upon us if we stray too far from the cities. They capture children who wander off alone.*

*And you kill them?* Aleria asked. Perhaps it was this race of mammals who had sent the distress signal.

Nehinei nodded. *When we can. But that is a rare occurrence indeed. They are cunning, ferocious, and strong. We carry these knives in defense*—he indicated the quartz knives that were woven through his webbed garment—*but they are a poor defense at best. The most effective strategy is to avoid the Rautgut entirely.*

*They are called Rautgut?*

*Yes, and pray you never see one—although, here, near the suma beds, we may. Like us, the Rautgut crave sumati. They try to steal it from the sumati-barss. Sometimes they succeed.* He shook his head. *A bad business.*

*Why?*

*Sumati-barss are a breed apart. They live alone, value their independence. They do not give up their hard-won sumati without a fight.*

*And the Rautgut give them that fight?*

*We assume so. No sumati-barss who have been attacked by Rautgut have lived to tell the tale.*

*Then how do you know it is the Rautgut who have attacked?*

*The evidence remains—the suma that they have destroyed, the taste of blood in the water. The Rautgut are destroyers.*

Aleria was about to ask what the Rautgut looked like when Nehinei pointed to the ocean floor beneath them. There amid the rolling hills on the bare mud bottom lay a huge cluster of giant clams—the largest Aleria had ever seen. Each could easily have contained a small cottage.

There was a kind of reverent silence about the suma grove, like an ancient redwood forest back on Earth. And indeed there was a parallel; as Nehinei explained, the suma were as old as the planet itself.

*No one knows how old they are*, he told them all, for Aleria had turned on the transponder so that she could be in touch with Houston and the telepathically mute Jemall. *No one knows how they reproduce. Perhaps all the suma have been here since the beginning of time. It is an offense on Kahiko to kill any mollusk, for it might someday grow into a giant suma. We have no way of knowing, since it cannot happen in our lifetime. But without the suma, there would be no sumati—and without the sumati, surely we would all die.*

*Interesting,* Aleria noted and was about to comment further when a tall Kahikan who strongly resembled Nehinei approached them.

*Lucky it's you, fenoki-spawn,* the newcomer told Nehinei, affectionately grasping Nehinei by the upper arms. *I would not tolerate anyone else bringing such an entourage into my territory.*

Nehinei looked around. He had brought Aleria, Rosmer, and Jemall—but the six mermaids had followed at a respectful distance.

*What are these creatures?* the newcomer asked.

*You didn't listen to the broadcast last night?*

*I seldom listen to broadcasts. At least, I don't pay them any attention.* He stopped to consider a moment. *I remember now. These are the visitors from beyond the lahnee?*

Nehinei nodded. *Judge Aleria Farrell, who will decide if we may join the Confederation. Her assistants, Jemall and Rosmer.* He turned to his guests. *This is my brother, Maikee,* he told them.

*You are sumati-barss?* Aleria asked.

*What's that?* hissed Jemall and Houston through the transponder.

*Sumati-gatherer,* she hissed back. *Shhh.*

*Yes,* replied Maikee. *I tired of the trappings of nobility. My brother may continue his princely duties if he chooses. I prefer to spend my days here alone with the giant suma.*

*You're a prince?* Aleria gasped.

Nehinei shrugged. *Why else would I be escorting guests around Kahiko or greeting trade missions? It would be just as easy to swim and sleep and conjoin at will, like everyone else, since no one on Kahiko really needs to work.*

*A prince must deal with the babble of schools of Kahikans, in the cities and on the rakun,* Markee added. *I prefer the silence of the suma.* Then he said curiously, *I presume you had a reason for disturbing that silence with your presence?*

While Nehinei explained Aleria's fact-finding mission to his brother—as he understood it; he still didn't know about the appeal from the unknown species—Aleria pondered the problem of her personal involvement with a prince of the people she was to evaluate. If, as in many societies, the prince was the embodiment of the state, she had seriously compromised her impartiality. And Nehinei's talent for broadcasting posed another problem; the whole planet would be privy to the intimate details of her relationship with the Kahikan. This might well appear to be a conflict of interest, if in fact it didn't actually constitute one—a realization that gave her pause.

Unfortunately, the Kahikan was extremely attractive. So was his brother, who resembled him greatly, except that his coloration leaned more towards the green. Maikee's eyes, Aleria noticed, were a pale green that so resembled the Kahikan waters that looking into them was almost like looking into the cool, clear depths of a forest pool. So like the waters that surrounded them were those eyes that for an instant Aleria had the uncomfortable sensation that she was looking straight through his head into the depths beyond.

But where Nehinei was supple and lithe, Maikee was well muscled, with an aura of physical power that was easily distinguished from his brother's attitude of easy command. There was about Maikee an aloof surliness, not at all like Nehinei's social grace.

Yet Maikee was, in his own way, just as attractive as Nehinei, the judge decided, and then put the thought from her mind. It would not do to become further involved with either of these two members of the royal house of Kahiko.

Maikee was not totally without social graces. He offered his visitors the hospitality of his home. This turned out to be the abandoned shell of a giant tortoise, connected by cartilage that had become fossilized so that it was hard as any rock.

*There is no coral near the suma beds*, he explained. *We brought this here from the tortoises' graveyard to serve as protection from the Rautgut.*

*The tortoises' graveyard?* Aleria asked.

*Yes*. Nehinei took up the explanation. *We have never known the giant tortoises. They died out long before Kahikans came to this ocean. But their shells all lie in a single place, as though they had gone there to die—or been carried there after death.*

*Curious*, remarked the judge. *And the Rautgut cannot get in? These openings seem fairly large.*

*The Rautgut will not come in. They seem to fear the tortoises. In our cities, we make the openings in the coral dwellings small enough to block the entry of the Rautgut. Even though their noses can penetrate, they cannot open their jaws*, the Kahikan prince continued.

*Then they are helpless. You can punch them in the snout, which is their most sensitive organ*, his brother added. *You can hit them hard enough to stun them—even kill them. But they won't even come near a tortoise shell*, he finished, great satisfaction in his voice.

*What my brother has failed to inform you is that, while Rautgut won't come near a tortoise shell, they will circle it until you come out,* Nehinei smiled. *But then, there is no reason to come out, except to gather sumati.*

*The a process that you have come to witness,* Maikee noted. *And one of my suma is about to open. Come and watch the gathering.*

*His suma?* Aleria narrowcast at Nehinei. *How does he come to own them?*

*He has staked a claim on this bed. He may mine it as long as he lives. Then it reverts to the crown to bestow upon the next person who seeks to claim it—provided he is not suspected of foul play in getting rid of the previous owner.*

Aleria nodded. So princes sat in judgment on their fellows. Then Nehinei's job was not so different from hers. Apparently, broadcasting his sexual adventures did not lower Nehinei in the eyes of his subjects. She asked Nehinei about that.

*Oh, on the contrary,* he told her. *The more innovative and pleasurable your conjoinings, the more respect you garner. He who has the loudest voice and the most audible broadcast technique will never be forced to abandon his throne.*

Aleria made a wry face. Power was, by her standards of privacy, expensively achieved on Kahiko.

Nehinei did not allay her discomfort when he hastened to add that she had made a favorable impression on his subjects through the broadcasts, as had Rosmer and Jemall. Aleria was pondering the ramifications of that piece of information when they arrived at the suma bed.

Sure enough, one of the giant clams had begun to open. Maikee whistled sharply, and a troop of kolenya appeared. Aleria realized with surprise something she had not noticed the night before: the kolenya were not true octopi; they had *nine* tentacles, arranged in three groups of three.

She soon became aware of the advantage of such an arrangement as the kolenya jockeyed for the chance to help mine the sumati. Two of the larger ones came to the fore. The others hauled up two massive coprolites from the ocean floor.

They waited in silence—Nehinei, Maikee, their guests, the mermaids, and the kolenya—as the shell of the giant suma began to yawn. Wider and wider it opened. When at last it had reached what he had determined was the maximum aperture, Maikee whistled again.

The sound cut through the water, and the two chosen kolenya bounded forward. Each hurled itself into one corner of the shell, just beside the hinge, and held it open, with three tentacles grasping the upper shell and three holding the lower.

The suma at once began to close its valves, but the kolenya strained valiantly to keep them apart. The other kolenya raced up to each side, bearing the huge coprolites. (Aleria suddenly wondered if those giant coprolites could have been left by the long extinct tortoises; it would have taken a creature of that enormity to produce such wastes.) Each of the two kolenya within the suma's shell reached out and grabbed a great rock with its three free tentacles, and jammed it into the hinge.

The suma at once began to generate a quantity of viscous liquid as it tried to rinse away the barriers that kept it from closing. Maikee moved in, quick as a dartfish, and gathered a fine nacreous powder into an empty, gourdlike shell, then clapped a flat shell, much like a sand dollar, across its open end and bolted from the jaws of the suma.

He had barely escaped when the clam succeeded in

forcing the coprolites out of its hinges. It snapped shut with a force that could have taken a man's leg off—or cut a good-sized fish in two.

Aleria, Jemall, and Rosmer jumped back in a reflex reaction, although they were nowhere near enough to have been in any danger. The two Kolenya had escaped by inches.

*That was close*, the dolphin breathed.

*It wasn't really*, Nehinei laughed. *He was showing off for his visitors. Maikee knows the suma—he had plenty of time.*

*Don't give away my secrets, brother*, Maikee laughed genially, *especially in front of the pretty female.*

Aleria blushed, but Maikee was paying no attention to her. He was lavishing affection and approval—and a number of small prawns—on his kolenya as rewards for a job well done.

At last, he took up his shell container of sumati and held it up for them to see. *The most valuable commodity in the realm*, he told them, *but to me, it's even more valuable, for it gives me an excuse to leave the duties of my royal family to my brother, and to live here in splendid isolation, far from the babble of the populated areas.*

They were admiring the translucent shell, nearly full of pearly powder, when a giant shadow, then another, blocked out the dim light from above.

*Rautgut!* cried Nehinei.

*They must have heard my whistle*, Maikee grimaced. *They know I've made a harvest.* He glanced up. *There are quite a number of them. They probably mean to attack.*

*What'll we do?* Aleria demanded, more shrilly than she had intended.

Maikee shrugged. *Take cover, of course. Quick—into the tortoise!*

# Chapter X

The tortoise shell proved commodious enough to hold them all, even the six mermaids and the gaggle of kolenya. There was plenty of room beneath the high-domed upper shell. Under water, one had to learn to think in terms of volume rather than floor space, Aleria realized.

Although bare of furnishings—what use had a Kahikan for chairs, tables, or beds in the nearly weightless world beneath the waves?—Maikee's home was richly decorated with draperies of red netting that hung from petrified-cartilage outcroppings on the inside of the tortoise shell. At several points, netting bags hung suspended. They were filled with the same kind of shells in which Maikee had collected the sumati. Hanging just beneath the highest point of the dome was a smaller cache of shells, filled shells—a king's ransom in sumati, coin of the Kahikan realm.

Aleria was fascinated by the spaciousness of Maikee's shell dwelling. It was far more elegant than the coral tenements of the city she had visited with Nehinei. *Build thee more stately mansions*, she reminded herself. The ancient poet had been right about the elegance of living within a shell.

It now looked as though Aleria, Jemall, and Rosmer were about to take up residence in this one, something that had not been part of their plan here in Kahiko. Outside, at a respectful distance but near enough to seem ominous, the huge, black Rautgut circled hungrily. Apparently, it was going to be a long night—or week, or month.

*How long will they stay?* Aleria asked Maikee.

*Till they tire of waiting.*

*How long will that be?*

He shrugged. *Who knows? A week, maybe. Or a year. I've waited them out before.*

He pointed out, then, that enough krill floated by so that they wouldn't lack for food. The same currents that brought the krill carried wastes away. There was ample space so they wouldn't crowd each other. And, if they grew bored, he certainly had plenty of sumati.

Aleria was still in the dark about the function of sumati. Nehinei had spoken often of "the throes of sumati," but had never elaborated on just what he meant by that. Though "throes" were pangs, or twinges, somehow Aleria got the impression that sumati was pleasurable, rather than painful. Or was it a little of both?

She was about to ask when Rosmer swam over, apparently quite distressed.

*Have they given you any idea how long we'll have to stay here?* he asked her, using a telepathic whisper.

*Maybe an hour, maybe a year. But aside from the fact that we're supposed to be conducting an investigation, it doesn't matter. We're safe, and we have no pressing needs that can't be satisfied here.*

*I do*, Rosmer informed her.

*Oh, I know you miss your Ring, Rossy, but you can manage without them a little longer. I'm here. I'll augment with you.*

*That's not the problem*, the dolphin protested.

*Well, then, what is?*

The dolphin looked miserable. *I've got to get out of here*, he narrowcast.

*Why?*

*I can't breathe.*

*Oh, Rosmer. Claustrophobia is a state of mind. You can handle it*, she reassured him.

*I'm not claustrophobic*, he virtually screamed at her. *I'm telling you I can't breathe!*

Everyone else in the shell turned to stare at the two of them, but Rosmer paid no attention. *Look, I've got to surface for air sooner or later—preferably sooner—or I'll drown. And I can't get through that siege force out there. Do something, please?*

It was only then that Aleria remembered that dolphins did not have gills. They surfaced to breathe, just as whales did.

*Well, we'll just have to get you out of here and to the surface.* Aleria smiled reassuringly and gave him a little pat on the side. *I guess that means dispersing the Rautgut.*

*Just like that?* Maikee asked sarcastically. *Do you realize how many of them there are out there?*

Aleria, preoccupied with checking the reservoir of her blaster, merely shrugged. *Couple of dozen, maybe?*

*A couple of dozen?* Maikee's telepathic voice rose to screaming volume. *Nehinei, your friends are crazy. But if anything happens to them while they're guests in my home, I'm the one who's going to look bad.* He glanced at Jemall, who had pulled out his swords and set them down on the lower shell of the tortoise. *Tell them, Nehinei. Knives do not penetrate the hide of the Rautgut, even knives as large as that, even knives made out of—whatever those are made out of.*

*Those aren't knives, they're swords*, Jemall mumbled absently. He was concentrating, hard; Aleria noticed that his forehead had that funny little wrinkle it sometimes got when he needed to block out distractions.

He flexed his long, four-jointed fingers once, twice, a third time, then mumbled something out loud, which was lost in a cascade of tiny bubbles. Again the silvery fingers flexed, extended—and the swords were gone. In their place lay a blaster rifle with a full-power magazine.

*How'd he do that?* Maikee asked of no one in particular.

*I don't know*, Nehinei replied, *but he does it all the time*.

*Well, a club won't work either*, Maikee told him petulantly.

*That isn't a club.*

*What is it?*

*You'll see.* Nehinei had seen blasters in use, but when he broadcast his memory of the incident with the fenoki, Maikee merely shrugged and turned away.

*You're all crazy*, the sumati-barss sighed.

Aleria and Jemall had taken up positions at the two entrances that must once have provided room for the tortoise's front legs. Nehinei grabbed his brother and pulled him over to the broad neck opening.

*Watch*, ordered the Kahikan prince.

Jemall put his blaster rifle to his shoulder. Aleria braced her gun across an extended forearm to steady it against the gentle currents. She glanced at the bailiff and nodded, just once.

A thin beam of light shot from each blaster, hitting the

nearest two Rautgut squarely on their noses. They stopped swimming and lay motionless in the water, apparently stunned. The others seemed to pull back just for a second. Then four of them, huge and black, came from behind and advanced toward the tortoise, jaws open, teeth bared.

Their awful mouths were completely filled with teeth, at least six rows of them on each jaw, arranged like bowling pins but obviously razor-sharp. The Rautgut hesitated a moment, as though weighing whether or not to come closer to the tortoise. Then the two who had been hit, obviously leaders, snapped out of their stupor.

One of them gave a mighty roar. The others turned toward it as though to verify that only its pride had been wounded. Ascertaining that, they began to advance on Maikee's home.

*Terrific*, muttered its owner. *They're so angry that they've forgotten to be afraid of the tortoise shell.*

*Shh, it's okay.* His brother made an attempt to placate him.

*That's all right for you to say*, Maikee complained. *You don't have to live here with a horde of Rautgut who aren't afraid of your house anymore.*

*Shh, it's okay*, Nehinei repeated. *Just watch.*

As the Rautgut advanced, Aleria and Jemall made adjustments on the power settings of their blasters.

*Stunning didn't warn them off*, Aleria observed. *How hard do we have to hit them, do you think, to kill them?*

*Don't bother with lower settings*, Jemall advised. *It's more efficient to disintegrate them.*

Aleria nodded. *You're probably right.* She really hated to disintegrate any living thing, but it was beginning to look like a choice between the Rautgut and the group hiding out in the tortoise shell. *It's them or us*, she thought grimly.

The Rautgut drew nearer, and Aleria could see that they appeared to be a cross between giant whales and open-jawed sharks—the more frightening for the rows of sharklike teeth that covered their palates like baleen plates. *They have the worst characteristics of each creature*, she thought to herself. And they were obviously carnivorous!

*The range is good*, she called to Jemall through the transponder connection. *Now!*

They both opened fire, and the two front Rautgut disappeared. But their companions kept right on coming; Aleria and Jemall wiped out the next two the same way.

The fifth and sixth—the ones that had been stunned by the earlier blast—suddenly froze where they swam. They looked to the left, to the right, above, below. They turned to look at the Rautgut assembled behind them. Then they broadcast a very primitive telepathic image to their comrades who had been ahead of them: *Where are you?*

There was, of course, no answer.

The Rautgut called out again, twice more. Then they turned back to the rest of their tribe and broadcast an image that clearly translated to "Now you see them, now you don't"—along with considerable puzzlement.

From the back of the mass of Rautgut, an ancient, graying female made her way to the two leaders. She broadcast a single telepathic image—a giant tortoise with flame-red eyes and breath of fire. The others turned to look once more at the tortoise shell.

The female Rautgut broadcast the image once more. The others took it up, a kind of agreement. Then, slowly, respectfully, cautiously, the Rautgut backed off, away from the tortoise.

When they had achieved what they apparently agreed was a point distant enough for them to take their eyes safely from the tortoise, the entire herd turned tail and fled.

Aleria had never heard a telepathic cheer before. Now the broadcast waves of huzzahs and hurrahs from her companions nearly bowled her over with their force. They reverberated inside her head and—from the way he was reacting—inside Jemall's as well.

A complaint from Houston, via the transponder, verified that fact. *Could you two please turn down the volume? All that whoopee-ti-yi-yi is making my circuits vibrate.*

*Sorry,* Aleria told him.

*It isn't you,* the ship informed her. *It's him.*

Aleria turned to Jemall, who had been standing dumbfounded, caught in the telepathic waves of adulation. Now he smiled sheepishly and apologized through the link, toning it down to moderate the volume of the cheering he was receiving from the telesending Kahikans, who were not the least bit reticent about expressing their happiness at the rout of the Rautgut.

All except Maikee. He had begun by mumbling to himself, *How'd they do that?* Then he had grabbed his brother by the shoulders and demanded to know how the visitors had destroyed the Rautgut. He was still shaking Nehinei and reiterating, *How, how?* when Aleria swam over to intercede.

*Maikee?* She touched his shoulder to get his attention.

He ignored her.

*Maikee!* This time she virtually screamed it.

He stopped shaking Nehinei and turned to the visiting Earthwoman, who stepped backward quickly to put herself beyond his reach. But he made no move toward her.

Instead, he asked her almost plaintively, *How did you do that?*

Aleria laughed out loud, causing herself to become encased in a cascade of tiny bubbles. *I couldn't begin to explain it so that you'd understand what I was talking about. You have to start with the concept of fire.*

*Fire?*

Nehinei, recovered from Maikee's assault, threw his brother the mental image of his experience with the magnifying glass. Aleria picked up on his narrowcast; it was like living the event on the shores of Rix all over again. Still, Maikee remained skeptical.

*I find that hard to believe,* he grumbled stubbornly.

*Well, do you believe what you just saw with your own eyes?* Nehinei countered.

Reluctantly, Maikee conceded that the blaster bolts might have been a form of fire rather than magic—but he still held to the notion that fire might itself be a form of magic.

Aleria had no real arguments to counter this. Fire that functioned under water was indeed magical if you didn't understand the scientific principles that made it work. She had a little trouble with some of the concepts herself; how much more difficult would they have been had she not grown up accepting the wonders of modern science?

*What about shape-changing?* Maikee wanted to know. *Isn't that a form of sorcery?*

*Not really,* Aleria shrugged. She concentrated on sending the sumati-barss a series of images: atomic structure, molecules, basic cellular building blocks. It was quicker than a verbal explanation would have been, but met with much the same skepticism she imagined she would have encountered from anyone being introduced to those concepts for the first time.

Maikee finally accepted her explanations for lack of any others that sounded more convincing. Aleria glanced up and saw that Jemall, surrounded by his admiring mer-harem, was in the process of transmuting his blaster rifle back into the swords without which he seemed to feel undressed. Rosmer, of course, had bolted for the surface as soon as the coast was clear.

The bailiff wore a rather disgusted expression.

*What's the matter?* Aleria asked him through the transponder link.

*I used up too much energy hitting those Rautgut with the blasters. Now I don't have enough substantial matter to recreate both swords. And I can't explain it to anyone, since no one can hear me.*

Aleria nodded, understanding. She flashed an image at the others: *Jemall needs coprolites and shells.*

All of the Kahikans disappeared, along with the kolenya to return almost instantly with enough shells and coprolites to build a small house.

*Feast or famine*, the Acetan muttered, and set about restoring his swords. With far more material than he needed, he made Aleria an extra power magazine for her blaster, then turned the rest into seven strings of pearls, one for Aleria and the others for the mermaids.

The Kahikans appeared fascinated by the pearls. They kept rubbing their webbed fingers across them, feeling their texture. A mermaid even tried to bite into one.

*Almost like sumati*, Nehinei breathed.

Maikee, too, was impressed. *What are these?* he wanted to know.

*Don't you have pearls on Kahiko?* Aleria was astounded. She flashed them a series of mental images to explain the creation of pearls from irritants that found their way inside the shells of mollusks on Earth.

*Perhaps that is what the sumati are—tiny pearls*, ventured Nehinei. *They shine with the same kind of glow, and they are made by the suma.*

*But do pearls have the same power?* Maikee asked.

*I wonder.* His brother turned to Aleria and Jemall. *Do you ingest these?*

*Ingest?* the visitors gasped. *Pearls?*

The Kahikans heard only Aleria's voice, but Houston heard them both. *There have been races who used ground pearls as a potion*, he advised them. *But the substance has no curative or even, as once was hoped, aphrodisiac powers.*

Aleria said as much to the Kahikans, who appeared momentarily startled, then smiled.

*Perhaps it has no effect on their race*, Nehinei told his brother. *Then again, many legends have a basis in fact. If pearls had this power according to their legend—*

*If pearls have this power, Jemall has put me out of business*, Maikee snarled. *There is more pearl powder in those necklaces than I could glean in a lifetime of sumati-gathering.*

*Maybe they don't have the power*, Nehinei said. *We could try ingesting some.*

*If it worked on us and not on them, we would be most impolite*, his brother reminded him. *To engage in a sumatiansa, while our guests could only watch, would be very rude.*

*Oh, I don't think they'd just watch*, Nehinei smiled knowingly.

*Well, I think we should offer them the real thing. They drove off the Rautgut. We owe them that.*

*Owe us what?* Rosmer asked, making a flamboyant entrance through one of the hind-leg openings of the tortoise.

*True Kahikan hospitality*, Maikee replied. *Come, we will share sumati together.*

His tone was so reverent that Aleria didn't dare to venture even a polite protest. The sumati-barss swam rapidly to his cache near the dome, removed one small, filled shell, and returned to the very center of his tortoise-shell home. The mermaids, Nehinei, even the kolenya drew close, swimming in a reverent orbit around him.

*Come*, he told Aleria, Jemall, and Rosmer. *Share.*

*Analyze it*, the judge ordered the bailiff hastily. *Is it poisonous?*

Jemall concentrated for a moment. *Doesn't appear to be*, he told her through the link. *It's organic, but not bacterial. Seems basically inert—but then, those clams are pretty inert, aren't they? I understand that each opens only once every fifty standard years!*

*You're sure it won't hurt us?*

*The only way to be sure is to test it—which is not the best procedure. But it looks as though refusing would be extremely rude.* He shrugged. *It doesn't seem to contain any recognizable poisons. I'd say we should give it a try.*

*All right*, Aleria agreed. Her curiosity about sumati had been piqued long ago. She had been about as cautious as she was going to be. *Come on, Rosmer.*

But the dolphin was way ahead of her. He had already joined the charmed circle around Maikee.

*Come. Share. Come*, the Kahikan called, and Aleria heard echoes of the way his brother had hummed to her, in the cavern beneath the coral citadel. *Come. Come.*

The others took up the cry in low, melodious voices. *Come. Come.* And then, as they swam closer to him,

Maikee placed a tiny portion of the sumati in the open mouth of each.

*Almost like a religious communion*, Aleria noted privately. She opened her mouth and let Maikee place a portion of sumati on her tongue.

When all the mermaids, Kahikans, and their visitors had partaken, Maikee helped himself, then handed the sumati shell to a waiting koleno. This koleno withdrew a small portion, shared it with the other kolenya, then shot to the top of the dome, replacing the shell among the others in the cache. Last to partake, the koleno joined his fellows in the outer ring of their charmed circle.

The mermaids and the other Kahikans did not appear to chew or swallow the sumati. They were humming, humming, letting the sumati dissolve in their mouths. Aleria felt her own tiny portion of sumati dust dissolving on her tongue. It produced an odd, vibrating sensation along the nerves of her mouth, almost as though the sumati—and her mouth—were alive. Almost without volition, she too, began to hum in chorus with her hosts.

The electric tone of the humming seemed to fill her soul, making her entire body tingle with temptation and desire. She felt herself moving, almost involuntarily, closer and closer to Maikee, their host, the hub of the circle.

The Kahikans were beginning to vary their body colors. A rainbow of iridescent blues and greens and mauves and silvers glowed before her eyes—the silver of Jemall, the silvery white of the dolphin's underside, the iridescent greenish mauve of Nehinei, the pale nacreous blue of his brother. The waters themselves seemed to be turning colors, all the colors of the Kahikan rainbow, the watery colors of the blue end of the spectrum. Green. Blue. Indigo. Violet. Ultraviolet.

She was *seeing* ultraviolet! But that was impossible! The waters around them were changing colors even as the Kahikans did, and then the waters themselves were humming, humming, charged with their growing passion. And Aleria was one with the waters, one with the humming, one with all the others—Jemall, Rosmer, Maikee, Nehinei, all six of the mermaids, even the kolenya. Humming, flowing, soaring, she was merging with them all, physically, emotionally, telepathically—feeling their sensations, all of them, even as she experienced her own, even as they, too, felt hers. The humming sounded in her ears like a symphony, and she was helpless against its lure. She could only follow the music blindly, helplessly, as it rose to a crescendo on its way to what must certainly be the ultimate coda.

# Chapter XI

Merged in an augmentation, their minds open to one another and the dolphin Ring, neither Medina nor Levis was prepared for the assault of sensations that suddenly filled their minds, possessed their bodies. For that matter, neither were the dolphins of the Ring. Poised on the brink of an attempt at interstellar telepathic communication, they were caught with all of their defenses down.

Incredible sexual sensations swept over them in waves, one after another, unceasing, each one stronger than the one that had gone before. With their minds so turned on, their bodies couldn't help but follow.

In the end, only the fact that they were still outside the dolphins' tank, with just their arms inside to amplify their contact, kept Levis and Medina from quite literally drowning in sexual excess, for they were helpless against the mental onslaught; their bodies moved against, within, around each other with not the slightest exercise of caution. Had they been in the tank, it would not have occurred to them to surface for air.

Levis had no memory of how or when they had removed their arms from the tank, stripped off the coveralls that they, like all workers on the monitoring station, wore, and fallen into a tangle on the floor. He didn't worry until afterward about the unlocked door, or about the possible consequences if anyone had walked in on them; they were, after all, in a room that was open to the public, and they were on duty as well. Levis hadn't even considered the awkward consequences of sexual involvement with his supervisor. His brain wasn't working; he could think only of mermaids, of silver, of shimmering bluish-greenish-mauve, of hair the color of flame. His body followed where his mind had already gone. He needed Medina, wanted her. As he reached out blindly, one thought reverberated inside his skull: *I must have her, must be one with her.*

Not only his need for Medina but Medina herself was inside his mind, wanting *him*, needing *him*, merging with him, flame-haired—no, that was someone else—and fish-tailed—no, that was also someone else. The two of them became disembodied mouths and tails, bodies experiencing sensation upon sensation, organs that reached and organs that swallowed, hands and skin and scales, lungs and gills, a tangle of arms and legs on the waterlogged carpeting that surrounded the dolphin tank on the monitoring station, a thrashing circle of octopus tentacles within a giant tortoise, a writhing Ring of dolphins floating in a tank that floated in space.

That Ring had formed a physical as well as a mental ring, broadcasting their frustration at the absence of Orono females even as, caught up in the waves of sensation from Kahiko and from the two humans just beyond the glass walls of their tank, they found alternative means of exorcising the demons that suddenly seemed to possess them. They, too, were inside Levis's mind—or he was within theirs. And they were all one with Medina, with a transmuted, flame-haired judge and an amphibious Acetan, with Kahikans and mermaids and kolenya and krill and with the waters of Kahiko themselves, endless rivers running to the sea, endless waves crashing upon the shore.

When at last the broadcast stopped, Levis and Medina rolled apart and lay naked and panting on the soaked carpet. The dolphins, too, seemed to be trying to catch their breath. Too exhausted to screen their embarrassment from the two humans just outside the tank, the Ring seemed helpless to come up with any acceptable—at least to their minds—excuse for their behavior.

Carswell voiced their gravest concern. *We can only hope that this broadcast was limited to us and to Rosmer and his party on that distant planet. We can only pray that we did not augment it so that the rest of the universe could be privy to our private thoughts.*

Levis rolled over and staggered to the door on wobbly legs. As he fumbled ineptly with the lock, securing it against visitors until he and Medina could regain their coordination, he tried to reassure the Ring. "I don't think there was anyone in that link except the denizens of that water planet; we have apparently been unwitting participants in their orgy—but even carried away as we were, I think we would have sensed the presence of others."

*If we had merged with them, yes,* Sebrook agreed. *But if we were merely broadcasting—*

*If we were broadcasting at the same time we were merging with that transmission, we have just provided pornographic mental movies for the entire planet Earth—possibly for the entire universe.* Carswell completed his thought. *It is something we will never be able to live down.*

"Wouldn't you know if you'd been broadcasting?" Medina protested.

After a pause, Selmar spoke for all three dolphins. *Normally, we would. But in this instance—would you know, would you be able to reconstruct, all of your activities over the past—*he broke off, checked the chronometer, and grimaced—*several hours*? he finished, disgust in his mental voice.

*"Hours?"* Medina and Levis gasped in unison. They both turned to stare at the chronometer. It *had* been hours since they'd first entered this room containing the dolphin tank, hours since they'd told Kabeel they'd only be gone a short while.

"Oh god! Kabeel!" Levis groaned. "What'll we tell him?"

Medina shrugged. "We told him we were on the verge of a breakthrough in interstellar communications. I suppose we could tell him we broke through."

"Sure," Levis replied. "Then *you* can be the one to explain just what kind of breakthrough we've made."

Spreadeagled, flat on her back on the soggy carpet, Medina was obviously too exhausted to come up with any clever retort. Levis could see that and could empathize even without being linked to her. He was exhausted himself.

He had been leaning against a bulkhead for support. Now he smiled wryly at Medina. "If you have any suggestions as to what to tell Kabeel, let me know." Levis planned to use any excuse that would pacify Kabeel and set his own mind at rest. He was having a hard time rationalizing his recent actions.

But Medina, staring into space, didn't seem to have the energy to worry about it. "Maybe he already knows," she mumbled, and fell fast asleep.

Levis opened his mouth to protest, saw that it was useless, closed it. Then he, too, fell into an exhausted sleep.

Jedrek Kabeel did not know what had come over him. He only knew that he was suddenly subject to the kind of desperate sexual urgency he hadn't known since he was a teenager. He had been monitoring the receptors for Meltor and Ostego, who had claimed to have some pressing business with the damned dolphins, when he suddenly became aware of an almost painful need to relieve himself sexually.

He tried to concentrate on his job—their job—but watching the monitors was a passive task, and nothing much seemed to be coming in over them at present. He tried reading a random piece of mail, just to verify that the monitors were accurate, but the message he pulled turned out to be a steamy love letter. Reading it only made his need worse. He began to pace the room. Where the hell were Meltor and Ostego, anyway? They had told him they'd only be gone a short while.

Kabeel tried to watch the monitors but found himself staring into space, lost in fantasies about mermaids and long-legged redheads. At one juncture, he caught himself slack-jawed and drooling over his fantasies while the monitors clattered on untended.

The sublim monitor had begun to ring. That had brought him back to the real world. But when he checked it by putting his hand on the receptor plate—even though he wasn't much of a sensitive—he found that it only enhanced his feelings of arousal.

"Dammit," he muttered to himself. "Get a hold on yourself, Kabeel."

But the urge grew within him and at last, locking himself into the main monitoring room, he gave in to it and did just as he'd advised himself.

All over the planet Earth, people were giving in to similar sexual impulses. Coy virgins sacrificed their virtue, long-refused offers were suddenly accepted, politics suddenly really did create strange bedfellows. On that part of the planet where the sun shone overhead, lunch hours were stretched to their limits, but it didn't seem to matter; no one was making much attempt to accomplish business as usual.

In several minor provinces where insurgents had battled with reigning forces in a throwback to ancient barbaric ways, generals and rebels alike found it practical to make love, not war. Religious ascetics, who would scourge themselves afterward, yielded to irrepressible desires. In zoos around the world, the animals put on demonstrations that would have been quite educational had anyone been watching—but most humans were otherwise occupied.

Even the birds of the air and the fish in the sea gave in to temptation. Salmon began heading for their home streams. Peacocks spread their brilliant tails. Bees exhausted themselves rushing from blossom to blossom. And even hard-to-breed animals, like gorillas and pandas, decided to forgo their usual choosiness in the interests of copulation.

Nine months later a sudden and definite increase in the human population would be logged, but no one would give reasons for it, since each of those hit by the psychological onslaught from Kahiko that day assumed that it was just some private lapse of control.

No one thought to correlate the surge in the human population to the strange increases in animal and insect populations that occurred at various times that year, since the gestation periods of different creatures on Earth varied so widely. It was only years later that demographers would remark on the coincidence.

But not even the Orono, the most sensitive of sensitives, understood this sudden planetwide wave of horniness when it occurred. They only knew that lust had replaced logic even among dolphins, who normally controlled such impulses—when they chose to do so—without difficulty. Finding themselves reacting uncontrollably—like men—embarrassed them, and they avoided speaking of it afterward.

Hours—or was it days?—after her initiation to sumati, Aleria awoke tangled in the arms of Maikee and one of the mermaids. If she had thought—had hoped—the experience was a dream, the circumstance in which she found herself on waking disabused her of that notion. Had she really—? Well, she could understand partaking of Maikee's rough charms, so different from his brother's and yet so similar. She and Jemall had found themselves in orgies before, so this one was not, as the courts were wont to say, a case of first impression. Yet she could not remember ever having abandoned herself so completely to any sexual adventure. She might have blushed as she remembered some of the uses to which the kolenya had put their tentacles, and would have blushed even more deeply when she remembered the role played by the mermaids in all of this. But she had no embarrassment left, no blushes whatsoever, after bits and snatches of the entire scene came back to her, disconnected but quite distinct. Jemall, of course.

Maikee and Nehinei—well, why not? But both brothers at the same time? She had a little trouble with that.

The part that troubled her the most, in retrospect, was coupling with Rosmer—with a dolphin! Why that should trouble her more than the idea of kolenya or Kahikans, or even an Acetan, she wasn't sure, but trouble her it did—even though it had been wonderful, more wonderful than she had ever dreamed such a joining could be.

Ingesting the sumati had made emotional conjoining with the others as easy as physical conjoining. Even as she made love to Kahikan or Acetan, koleno, mermaid, or dolphin—even as she reached out to them, she was within them as they reached out for her. It was a strange, narcissistic kind of lovemaking, she reflected, yet it also brought an understanding she had never experienced before. To be truly one with your lover—or lovers—even as you knew their love—that was a wondrous feeling indeed!

As she floated within the tortoise shell, Aleria realized that this was an experience she had to know again. It was a need that gnawed at her psyche, grew like a hunger within her. She *would* know it again. She must!

Greedy for another chance to lose herself in the throes of sumati, she reached out and, with deft fingers, began to tease the sumati-barss awake.

*I want more*, she told Maikee as he began to respond to her ministrations. *Now*.

*Everyone always does*, he chuckled. *That's how I make my living*.

*Now*, she urged.

*Now*, came in echo in both of their minds. It was Rosmer, broadcasting a need even more intense than Aleria's, a need that was almost violent in its raw longing.

Maikee stretched slowly. *Maybe we shouldn't overdo it so soon. There's always tomorrow. Why exhaust ourselves?*

Aleria had to agree with the logic of resting before the next orgy. But her body didn't want to take the advice of her mind. She felt her legs itching to propel her to the top of the tortoise, her arms twitching for the chance to reach out for the cache of filled shells. *Just one more time today*, she cajoled, running her finger along what she now knew was the most sensitive edge of the Kahikan's gills.

*Please*, the dolphin begged. *Once more. Now.*

The desperation of his tone bothered Aleria. Did she, too, sound so frantic? Much as she didn't like to do it, she forced herself to exercise some restraint. *Perhaps it would be better to wait until we've got our strength back*, she suggested to Rosmer.

*No! Now!* The dolphin projected a need so raw that it broke through Aleria's defenses. *She* needed, too. Now. Now!

*This*, said a voice from the depths of her mind, *is too much.* The voice had a distinctly southern drawl, and it took Aleria a moment to recognize it as Houston's, quoting one of her favorite literary characters. Almost automatically, she began a retort about eavesdroppers—travel through interstellar space gave one the time to reread favored works often enough to memorize them. But Houston cut her off: *Eavesdroppers wouldn't be eavesdropping if you'd remember to shut down the link before embarking on such disgusting adventures.*

*Prissy, prissy*, she said sourly, hoping he'd catch her dual meaning. *Without the link, how would Jemall be able to communicate?*

*I did all right with Rosmer and the mermaids*, the bailiff retorted smugly.

*So I can shut it off?* Aleria offered.

*No!*

*I thought not.* She directed her thoughts back at the ship. *Why "Gone with the Wind"?* she asked him.

*Because I think you've had enough orgies for the time being. To quote Miz Scarlett—*

*I know, I know, tomorrow is another day.* She turned to the dolphin and suggested as much.

*No!* he protested. *Now!*

Aleria looked at him more closely. He seemed to be trembling, and if a dolphin could have doubled over, Rosmer would have done so. *Rossy, are you ill?* she asked, her concern evident.

*No*, he gasped. *Just—need.*

As Aleria thought about Rosmer's strange behavior, she became vaguely aware that her own body was reacting rather uncomfortably. Her arms tingled and, for the first time, the waters of Kahiko seemed uncomfortably cool. Her stomach felt just a bit queasy. And somehow she knew the cause—and that the cure of it was "hair of the dog," to use an old phrase—although why dog hair would imply "more of the same" was something that eluded her; language had certainly retained some strange expressions over the ages!

*I think you have a hangover, Rosmer*, Aleria advised the dolphin. Then, turning to Maikee, she formulated a mental picture of "morning after" and asked, *Am I right?*

The Kahikan threw her a different image, one that she rejected at first, then began to understand with rising horror. Sumati was addictive! But so quickly?

*That is unusual*, Maikee noted. *It normally takes multiple indulgences over a short time to develop a dependency such as Rosmer's—or even yours! Your Earth races must be particularly susceptible to it.*

This was not a statement guaranteed to produce peace of mind, Aleria reflected. *What about the Acetan?* she demanded.

Maikee shrugged. *Ask him.*

Aleria turned to Jemall and directed her thoughts to him through the link. *What did you think of the sumati?* she began cautiously.

*A good wine, but not a great wine.*

*What do you mean?*

*I've been to better orgies. The only really different facet of this one was being plugged in to your mind through the transponder. But, to tell you the truth, I couldn't follow most of what you were projecting. I think you overloaded the link. Maybe you overloaded your brain!*

*Watch it,* Aleria warned. *Don't forget who works for whom around here.*

*Sorry about that, chief.*

*I thought I asked you not to call me chief,* she growled. *You mean the sumati didn't affect you?*

The Acetan merely shook his head.

With Jemall unaffected and Rosmer already addicted, Aleria explored her own reactions carefully. She realized that she was feeling the stirrings of nascent dependency—and not just a psychological one.

*What about you Kahikans?* she demanded of them. *Are you addicted to it?*

*Some of us. Some can't even try sumati without needing it, more and more, all the time, every day. But some of us just use it when it's around.*

*Like an alcohol dependency,* Aleria reflected. You have

to be susceptible to it. What do you do for dependent Kahikans?

Maikee looked at his brother.

*Not much*, the prince admitted. *Some of them can just quit. That's one of the reasons we convey—so that they can have the sensations of sumati without having to partake of it.*

*And the others? The ones who remain dependent?*

*That's why Kahikans work.*

Aleria stared at him.

*Well, why else?* he asked her. *There is nothing we need that the waters do not supply—except sumati. Those whose need for sumati is greatest—or their families—work the rakun or carve knives or coral. They earn enough to trade for sumati.*

Aleria turned back to the sumati-barss. *If you have no need for sumati, why do you work?* she demanded pointedly. *What do you gain?*

*Three things*, he smiled. *My solitude. And all the sumati I could ever want or need.*

*And?*

*Obligation.*

*What?*

*Obligation.* He turned to his brother. *Explain it, Prince.*

Nehinei sighed. *I told you that the sumati beds belong to the crown. So it has been since the beginning of our people's memory. And—*

*And you get your cut?*

The Kahikan nodded. *It guarantees us a certain power—and a certain following among those who wish to align themselves with that power.*

*But you*—Aleria turned back to Maikee—*you gave up the trappings of power.*

*The trappings, yes. The power, no. I contribute to my family's power by mining sumati. That is in my interest. But it also maintains their obligation to me.*

The Kahikans were more machiavellian than she had given them credit for being, Aleria realized. What else went on inside those iridescent-scaled heads, she wondered, what else had they been screening? She was not a strong enough telepath to break through their blocks to find out; she would need Rosmer's help.

But the dolphin was a basket case (another expression whose origins eluded her). He was swimming in odd, irregular loops, quivering and occasionally jerking spasmodically.

Aleria turned back to the Kahikans. *What's the antidote?*

*Antidote?*

*The cure.*

*Oh, the cure.* Nehinei began to inspect the webbing between his fingers.

*The cure,* Aleria repeated.

*Yes, well—*

*The cure,* she demanded.

*Well*—Nehinei began.

*There isn't one,* his brother stated flatly.

Aleria was ahast. *You offered sumati to us, to strangers, knowing that?*

Nehinei looked away. Aleria, furious, dived out of the nearest opening in the tortoise shell and headed for the suma bed. She needed to control her anger. She needed to think. She needed a plan.

Aleria wanted sumati. She needed it, craved it even more intensely now that she knew she didn't dare try it ever again. *She* could fight her incipient addiction—but what about Rosmer?

The dolphin was a wreck. He'd have to have a fix while

the judge tried to figure out what to do for him. *Any suggestions?* she asked the bailiff and the ship through the link.

*Get me some; and I'll analyze it*, Jemall offered. *Maybe I can make some synthetic sumati for Rosmer to use when he gets like this.*

*Methadone*, the ship told him.

*Methadone?*

*Actually, methadone hydrochloride.* The ship flashed them his background information on the substance. *During the later Middle Ages, they used it as a substitute for heroin, back before they developed the antidote for heroin dependency.*

*If I can figure out what sumati is composed of, I should be able to transmute some coprolites into a sumati methadone*, Jemall hazarded.

Aleria nodded. *I'll get you some sumati*, she promised him. *And I'd better get Rosmer some of the real thing to tide him over.* She turned to the Kahikans who, with Jemall, had joined her in the suma bed. *I'll need some sumati for Rosmer until we can figure out what to do for him.* She glanced over at the dolphin, who was obviously in a bad way. *And some more, so that Jemall can analyze it.*

*It'll cost you*, Maikee told her.

*That will cost you!* Aleria did not take kindly to being threatened.

*Now, now*, Nehinei intervened. *The judge is our guest. And she is going to decide whether we should be admitted to the Confederation of Planets. Remember—glass? Cool fire to light our way through the darkest waters? Blasters to force off the Rautgut—*

Maikee was reluctantly convinced, but still not inclined

to be generous. *Well, give her some of yours, then*, he snarled.

*I haven't any with me. I'll owe you.*

*You already do.*

*Dammit, Maikee, this is no time to start straightening out our accounting. Just give me my share of the last gathering—what you collected just before the Rautgut attacked.*

Maikee shrugged, then handed it over without a word. His brother took the partially filled shell and, immediately passed it to Aleria. *My gift*, he told her.

Aleria smiled wryly. *Apparently one should beware of Kahikans bearing gifts*, she muttered to Jemall through the link. Then she called to the dolphin, *Come and get it.*

Rosmer appeared at her side instantly. *Need. Now.* Could dolphins cry? This one was nearly weeping.

The judge took an infinitesimal portion from the shell for him, then quickly gave the rest to Jemall. *Take it*, she commanded. *And get to work.*

The Acetan saluted mockingly, then headed swiftly for Rix before she could comment on his actions.

Aleria turned to the dolphin. *Open your mouth*, she ordered. He did. She placed the tiny portion on his tongue, then waited to see what its effect would be.

For just a moment, Rosmer did not react at all. He hovered there beside Aleria in the still Kahikan waters, moving barely enough to keep afloat. Then he began to broadcast faint waves of sexual fantasy—of mermaids and female dolphins, kolenya, small whales, and even a fleeting image of a metal-studded Rautgut female.

It was clear that Rosmer preferred females, something Aleria would have expected. But he was also into S and M, she realized with a jolt. *Oh, well—chacun à son goût*, she reminded herself, wondering even as she did so just what everyone's personal taste had to do with an inflammation of the big toe. However did such strange phrases find their way into Confederation Standard speech? she marveled.

Then Rosmer's quick movement shook her from her reverie, and she sidestepped as quickly as she could. She still had a tendency to use movements she had become accustomed to on Earth and in space, movements that were hampered by the resistance offered by the water. Now such movements seemed a ponderously slow way to carry her to safety behind a giant clam as the dolphin began to advance toward her.

He didn't seem to be Rosmer. He seemed instead to be some stranger inhabiting his own private erotic world, repeatedly living out his fantasies as he rubbed himself against every object in his path—the ocean floor, a stray flatfish, a couple of curious kolenya, and even the ancient and impassive suma that nested here in this strange, silent colony.

The dolphin swooped and soared and looped and glided through the shimmering waters, then finally impaled himself on the nether end of the tortoise shell, making a most interesting use of the small aperture through which the giant turtle's tail had once projected.

Inside the tortoise shell, the six Kahikan mermaids tittered in amusement. Aleria picked up on waves of telepathic delight—and she had to admit that their vision of Rosmer, since they could see only one small part of him from inside the shell, was not the visage that he normally presented to the world. The vision was too tempting for them to resist. One of the mermaids suddenly swam closer and began to caress his projecting organ with various parts of her own anatomy, conveying as she did so.

This was Aleria's first experience at picking up on a conveyed reaction in which she wasn't participating. The mermaid had merged mentally as well as physically with the dolphin and was broadcasting his experiences as well as her own through the waters of the planet. It was rather like watching a holographic movie, a video in three dimensions, perhaps in three dimensions squared! Depending on how completely one yielded to the broadcast, one could watch it from a distance or close up, or one could experience the feeling of actual participation. The Kahikans had developed voyeurism to new heights—or was it depths?

The dolphin seemed to be insatiable, but participation in two orgies in quick succession had taken its toll on his stamina and staying power. He pulled himself free of the tortoise shell, made a few soaring loops around the area, and then came to rest among the giant bivalves of the suma bed.

The broadcasting stopped, and Aleria sighed with relief. Sharing the experiences of the dolphin and his mermaid partner, not to mention the tortoise shell, had quickened her pulse, and the judge knew that it wouldn't take much urging to get one of the waiting Kahikans to scratch the psychological itch that was growing within her. But she also knew that this was a rare opportunity to observe the effects of sumati on another being without losing herself to it, so she held her desires in check.

She was just getting her heartbeat to return to normal when the dolphin began to stir, then to writhe among the suma. Aleria hoped he was not about to enter into repeat performance. Satiety was making sex almost painful for him at this juncture, and he had conveyed the pain, too. But the dolphin was not responding sexually.

He suddenly pulled himself away from the suma and

began to swim rapidly backward by fanning his tail slowly up and down. He seemed absolutely horrified by something, and Aleria caught herself casting a wary eye about for the appearance of Rautgut or fenoki.

She saw neither, and was about to dismiss Rosmer's reaction as some kind of hallucination when he let out a horrible scream, both mentally and vocally. Dolphins, when not communicating by telepathy, normally squeaked, clicked, and chirped, but Rosmer's cry was a lowing, painful groan.

*No!* the dolphin called out in his mind. He seemed to be trying to deny something so awful that he couldn't even visualize it, which effectively kept Aleria and the others from picking up the image in his mind. *No. Oh, no. Oh, no.*

Lost in his agony, Rosmer swam past Aleria almost blindly. *No*, he cried again. *No*.

Wearing a look of horror, he shot over the ridges that marked the edge of the suma bed, and out into the open waters of the great Kahikan sea.

Aleria stared after him numbly, trying to fathom the awful vision that could have prompted this uncharacteristic behavior. Then, suddenly, the two Kahikan princes swam up beside her.

*Why didn't you stop him?* Nehinei demanded.

*Why should I? He'll be okay. He was born in the ocean.*

*Not this ocean*, Nehinei pointed out.

*So?* Aleria asked, bewildered.

Maikee's explanation only added to her alarm. *Rosmer is headed the wrong way*, the sumati-barss told Aleria. *Into the wilderness, where the Rautgut live—and other creatures just as awesome and dangerous.*

*Only the most foolhardy Kahikans would ever venture*

*into those regions,* Nehinei added, *and even the most foolhardy would never travel through that territory alone!*

*How were we supposed to know that?* Aleria asked. *You could have warned us.*

*Who would have dreamed he would take off like that?* Nehinei protested.

*It isn't like him*, Aleria admitted. *He saw something—in his mind. Is sumati hallucinogenic?*

*No, just sensation-enhancing—at least, for Kahikans. But for off-worlders, who knows?*

*We haven't time to waste in speculation*, Maikee admonished. *We have to get that dolphin back into safe waters.*

*You're right*, agreed his brother. *Come on, Aleria. Let's go after him.*

The two of them grabbed her by the arms and pulled her clear of the suma bed. Then Maikee whistled for his crew of kolenya, posted half a dozen at the suma bed to protect it, and took off with the rest—and his brother and the visiting Confederation judge—in pursuit of the fleeing dolphin.

=Chapter XII=

The dolphin had a substantial head start, and it was only the link created by Aleria's augmentation training with him that enabled them to track him at all. He left a faint psychic trail of fear and loathing that only she—not even the Kahikans—could sense.

Aleria considered. Perhaps it was not the augmentation training but her initiation to sumati that had increased her psychic abilities—at least where those with whom she'd shared the substance were concerned. For she was discovering that her senses were keenly attuned to telepathic sensations from Maikee and Nehinei as well.

Unfortunately, Rosmer's psychic abilities had also improved. As Aleria and the Kahikans attempted to close in on him, he seemed to anticipate their every move, and the judge realized that, despite their screening, he was picking up on their telepathic discussions of how to catch him.

*He's reading everything we say*, she complained to the two Kahikans.

*But we're screening—what else can we do?* Nehinei protested.

Aleria pondered for a moment, then replied, *I have an idea. Come join me on the surface.*

They swam upward toward the bright mirror that marked the division between Kahiko's water and the air above them. As they neared the surface, Aleria opened the transponder channel to Houston and Jemall. *How're you coming with that methadone?* she asked the bailiff.

*I've almost got the sumati analyzed*, Jemall told her, *but I don't think you're going to like what I'm finding.*

Aleria cut him short, dismissing the details for the time being, still trying to put her craving for sumati out of her thoughts. She had more pressing problems—like catching that hysterical dolphin before the Rautgut, or something even more fearsome, got to him. *How soon can you join us?* she snapped.

*Give me a few more minutes. What's up?*

*I'll tell you when you get here. Bring a couple of extra blasters.* She cut off the transmission as she broke through the surface. After the dimness of the depths, the bright Kahikan sunlight made her blink. Still, it felt good to breathe the briny atmosphere like a mammal once again instead of getting her oxygen through the gills Jemall had given her.

Nehinei and Maikee surfaced beside her, shading their eyes with their webbed hands against the sun's glare on the water. She noticed that they seemed to be alone.

"Where are the Kolenya?" she inquired.

"I've posted them just below the surface to watch for Ratugut." Maikee's voice, which she had never heard before, was low and guttural. "We leave our nether parts unprotected when we tread water like this."

Aleria nodded, wondering why she hadn't thought of that. "Good idea."

Nehinei's voice, smoother than his brother's, was more pleasant to her ears. "Speaking of ideas, what was the idea you had that brought us up here?"

"The water is carrying our thoughts to Rosmer, but he won't be able to hear our voices if we talk up here. And I've got a plan."

"No matter what we plan now, we won't be able to communicate without Rosmer overhearing once we're back below the surface," the prince pointed out.

"That's part of the plan. Jemall and I can contact each other using the transponders. You won't be able to hear us, but neither will Rosmer."

"Then how will we know what to do?" Maikee wanted to know.

"Simple. I've asked Jemall to join us. You follow him and Nehinei will follow me. If we need to, we'll signal with our hands. I think we should try to slip up on Rosmer from both sides and trap him in some of that netting you wear."

"Sounds good," said Nehinei, "but we have very little with us—only what we're wearing. You may have it, of course, but that will leave us with no way to carry our knives."

"I'll have Jemall take care of that. He should be along shortly."

But they bobbed there on the surface for what seemed to Aleria to be much longer than the few minutes Jemall had promised. All this free time gave her too much opportunity to focus on the insatiable hunger that was welling up within her, a craving that would not be assuaged without more sumati. She knew that if it built long enough, she would be as helpless in her need as Rosmer had been in his. Impatiently, she reopened the channel to the bailiff. *Where are you?*

*On my way—with the synthetic sumati! There may be a problem with it, though—*

*I don't want to hear about it. Just get here,* she snapped.

*Hey, you can't expect me to cover twenty thousand leagues under the sea in ten minutes. I'm coming.*

*It isn't that far! Did you bring the blasters?*

*Yes, and a couple of blaster belts, too.*

Aleria sighed with relief. Now she wouldn't have any qualms about asking the Kahikans to surrender their garments. If he would only get here!

True to his promise, the bailiff popped to the surface beside them only moments later. Aleria took the two blaster belts from him and handed them to the Kahikans, who strapped them on and happily surrendered their red netting garments.

Jemall merged the edges of the two garments together to form one large net, then folded it up in accordion pleats that would unfold easily when he cast it out. Then, glancing about at the open sea, he announced, "I'll need something to weigh down the throwing edge."

Maikee, quick to comprehend, sent one of the kolenya to the ocean floor for coprolites. Jemall bound these into the edge of the net. Thus armed with net and blasters, the four of them set off once again in pursuit of the dolphin.

As they dived beneath the waters, Aleria was amused at the picture the Kahikans presented. They were now stark naked except for their blaster holsters, which they wore strapped across their hips and bound to one thigh. They had slipped their quartz knives under their belts over the opposite hip, and they presented a curious image that might have proved exciting to someone into whips and leather—if it hadn't been for those retractable organs of theirs. For, although the Kahikans' bodies were well muscled and brilliantly luminescent, the apparent absence of sexual organs made them appear as innocent as children.

Aleria shrugged. Appearances were deceiving. There was nothing innocent about the Kahikan royal family, or about any of the other Kahikans she had encountered in her tour of the planet. But she soon found it necessary to clear her mind of all thoughts of the Kahikans, for the psychic trail of the dolphin had faded and following it took all her concentration.

They were swimming now through waters very different from the more populous areas of Kahiko and different, too, from the area around the suma beds. She glanced down at the peaks of immense underwater mountains, the crevasses between them plunging to unfathomable depths. The jagged mountain ridges resembled lava cliffs, though there was no other evidence of volcanic activity on the planet.

They passed a colony of strange, translucent, tentacled creatures affixed to one bare peak. Maikee warned Aleria to keep away from them; their tentacles could shoot out great distances to grab passing prey, and their very touch brought instant paralysis.

Between the ridges, fish with markings like great luminescent eyes swam by in pairs. From a distance, they appeared to be the heads of giant, menacing monsters of the deep.

Now they passed a broad, dark well, sheltered by ragged cliffs, a deep, watery valley between the mountains. Something about that vast black lagoon made Aleria shudder.

It looked as though it might be populated by all manner of dread and dangerous creatures.

From the black lagoon they crossed more lava peaks with more of those luminescent eyes blinking between them, always following the psychic trail of the dolphin's fear and shame. Rosmer's flight led them farther into the wilderness to a vast rolling plain where, once again, sunlight could filter through the water. Off in the distance, Aleria could just make out the swimming dolphin.

He seemed to be slowing. She called out to him telepathically, but he did not respond, nor did he slow his pace. Aleria took off after him, with Jemall and the Kahikans at her heels broadcasting, *Rosmer, Rosmer, stop*.

But Rosmer did not stop, and the considerable lead he had over them seemed to be growing. The dolphin had the advantage of being a naturally strong swimmer, designed to move swiftly through the water. The Kahikans, too, swam powerfully, and Jemall's makeshift amphibious design was almost as effective. Now, in fact, as Aleria's party traversed the broad, flat plain, the four of them seemed to be gaining on Rosmer. Encouraged by the thought, they found it possible to redouble their efforts, but the dolphin swam on doggedly, keeping just beyond their reach.

Suddenly he swam into an area of shadow—or had the shadow moved to cover him? Glancing up, Aleria saw a small school of Rautgut hovering in the water above him, keeping pace with him as he swam.

The Rautgut looked as horrible as ever—humpbacked like a camel, but with the ferret face of a weasel, and, somehow, very like a whale. Aleria's first impulse was to flee. But where? Damn, she brooded, *there's never a tortoise around when you need one*. They would have to do battle with the Rautgut out in the open—and, from the ominous way the Rautgut were poised, it was obvious that there would be no avoiding a battle if they were to save the dolphin. Even at this distance, Aleria could pick up the hostile, hungry broadcasts of the giant sea scavengers as they hovered over their prey.

Aleria flashed to the Kahikans a telepathic image of how to handle a blaster. That was one good thing about telepathy—one picture was often worth a thousand words, and more. Easily comprehending, Maikee and Nehinei drew their weapons and came up close behind the judge and the bailiff. Aleria ordered them to set the blasters on disintegrate; as she adjusted hers, she heard the click of the other three being reset.

*Cover us*, Aleria told Jemall. Then she and Nehinei began to move in a wide circle toward the far side of the hovering Rautgut.

When she had reached a point that would give her an approach angle of about a hundred fifty degrees—no sense in moving in directly opposite and putting herself in Jemall's line of fire—she signaled, and all four of them began to move in, blasters at the ready. The two Kahikans kept a wary eye out for the approach of more Rautgut from the rear and sides. Then, on the judge's signal, she and Jemall fired in unison, taking out the two largest Rautgut.

The Rautgut were as baffled as they'd been during the battle at the tortoise shell, and before they could recover, Aleria and Jemall systematically eliminated the entire school, two at a time. The Rautgut, who were a little slow, made no move to retaliate.

In almost no time, the waters were clear of Rautgut. Aleria and Jemall turned their attention back to Rosmer— and realized that he was no longer fleeing. He seemed to have frozen right where he'd been when their battle with the giant predators had begun. Now he began to swim again, but in a series of erratic, almost tipsy patterns.

*Maybe he's having a sumati flashback*, Jemall suggested as they watched his odd behavior. But Aleria didn't think so. Rosmer's problem seemed a lot more serious than a flashback to an orgasm.

As they drew nearer, her suspicions were confirmed. The dolphin's skin seemed oddly mottled, and closer inspection revealed that it was covered with an odd pattern of large blisters. He was no longer attempting to flee and in fact made no protest when they threw their net around him. But it was only when Aleria drew up right beside him that she realized the seriousness of the problems besetting him.

Not only was he blistered and logy, but his bright eyes now were covered with a milky, opaque film. Aleria passed her hand in front of his face, and her worst fears were confirmed.

The dolphin was blind.

## Chapter XIII

Aleria felt a blind panic welling up within her. The dolphin was an Earth mammal, as was she; his body chemistry was far more like her own than were those of the Kahikans or her Acetan bailiff. His reaction to sumati had been more extreme than hers, it was true, but his addiction had been immediate—and, as she fought against her craving for the substance, Aleria realized that she shared his susceptibility.

Could the use of sumati have brought about Rosmer's present condition? If so, did the same fate lie in store for her?

She remembered how the once-dignified dolphin had been reduced to begging helplessly for more of the substance, and she found his craving for it easier and easier to understand. For as more and more time elapsed since her last exposure to it, every nerve in her body, every fiber of her being seemed to cry out for more sumati, in a blind hunger that she could barely contain. The intensity of that need disturbed her almost as much as its possible consequences.

Aleria stared at Rosmer, who floated limp and barely conscious in the softly billowing red netting. *Rosmer? Rossy?* She tried to reach out to him through the link they had forged, but he did not seem to recognize her. And when she tried to read his thoughts, she picked up only a jumble of disconnected emotions—fear, desire, and the all-encompassing need for sumati, a need she understood only too well. She probed further and was suddenly caught up in a wave of horror and shame, rooted somehow in more than just the dolphin's helpless need. And through it all—through the fear, the shame, the desire—ran the continuous current of another kind of longing, the dolphin's fierce homesickness for his Ring and for his home waters back on Earth.

Something about his craving for those home waters struck an odd chord in Aleria's memory—something that made the waters of Earth vastly different from those of Kahiko.

*Salt!* That was it. It suddenly came back to her—Rosmer's concern, when they had first arrived here, about the salt content of the Kahikan waters. What had he said? "Our skins become waterlogged. Our corneas cloud over."

*Jem*, Aleria virtually screamed through the transponder, *we've got to get Rosmer back to Rix, back to his tank. The Kahikan waters aren't salty enough for him. That's what his problem is!*

The big silver bailiff's pewter-colored eyes widened in disbelief, and Aleria knew what he was thinking. Surely the dolphin's actions weren't *all* based on a simple need for more sodium! But Jemall knew better than to challenge an order—even so indirectly phrased an order. He shrugged and took up a corner of the great red net in which they'd caught the unfortunate dolphin.

Aleria flashed a quick telepathic explanation to the Kahikans, who moved quickly to take up two more corners of the net as she hastened to pick up the fourth.

Alas, their progress back to Rix was anything but rapid. It wasn't easy to move through the waters with a semiconscious dolphin in tow. He was deadweight there in the net. That sleek body, designed to cut the water with such efficiency when he swam, now seemed to create the maximum possible resistance no matter how they tried to maneuver the net.

Their journey was further slowed by the need to surface periodically so that Rosmer could breathe. As soon as he'd taken in enough air, they would return to the depths again; they made far better time when they swam beneath the waves.

The waters in this part of Kahiko still seemed hostile and forbidding. Back over the lava mountains and the dark lagoon they retraced their earlier route, followed, always followed, it seemed, by those great staring eyes. Were they really just the markings on the hovering fish? Sometimes the eyes looked different; sometimes Aleria could not make out the fins and tails that she knew were there defining the bodies of those trompe l'oeil creatures. She found herself glancing over her shoulder with increasing frequency, just to reassure herself that their party was not being pursued by schools of hungry Rautgut, or by some other unknown creatures from the lava mountains or the black lagoon.

She chided herself for having too much imagination, but it was too easy to imagine evil in this murky world where friend and foe alike swayed and darted constantly in the gentle currents and where the things that did not move at all could prove the most deadly.

Had she been breathing instead of using her gills, Aleria would have sighed with relief when they finally reached Maikee's suma bed once more. It felt good to get back to civilization, even the edge of it. True, the Rautgut sometimes ventured into this part of the world, but here at least were coral towers and tortoise shells in which to take shelter from them. Somehow even Rautgut seemed less terrible now that Aleria and her companions swam in more familiar waters, populated by more recognizable hazards. Even the fenoki, confined as they were to the oki stands, seemed far less fearsome than the almost invisible rock creatures or the staring eyes or, worse, the unknown denizens of the lava mountains. "Here there be dragons"—Aleria remembered seeing those words on an ancient map of the seas of Earth. There had turned out to be no dragons in the unexplored waters of her home planet, but here on Kahiko, who could say?

This, however, was no time to panic or even to speculate. Aleria glanced at the dolphin, then urged her companions to pick up their pace. Across the vast, sandy plains, above the rakun, and over the coral capital, they redoubled their efforts to bring the ailing dolphin to Rix, where he could, perhaps, be healed. At last they reached the shallow waters that surrounded Kahiko's sole land mass. Jemall sprinted ahead to set up the dolphin's tank. As Aleria, Maikee and Nehinei hauled Rosmer up the sloping sand beach, they could see Jemall working his special form of magic. Using shells and coprolites and even sand from the beach, he expanded the tank. Then he filled it with water from the Kahikan sea. A flex or two of those odd Acetan fingers and the waters in the tank took on the proper chemistry.

Jemall leaped to help the others heave the dolphin into the tank. Out of the water, the small dolphin now seemed as heavy as a whale, and his limp body was almost impossible to maneuver. *Deadweight*, Aleria thought grimly, and then panicked at the thought and checked hastily to verify that the dolphin was indeed still alive.

He was, and he seemed to respond almost instantly to the greater salinity of the waters in the tank. He still looked terrible, but at least now he was surfacing and sounding on his own.

That was a relief, for Aleria had not figured out how to give artificial respiration to a dolphin. Now she slumped against the outside of the tank in exhaustion, too tired to fight her need for sumati any longer, too tired to care what the consequences of its use might be—and almost too tired to care whether her crying need for it could be, would be satisfied.

She turned to the bailiff. "Well, Jem, we can't do anything more for Rosmer. Why don't we check that artificial sumati you've created?

What a relief to use her voice instead of that damn transponder! But using her voice meant the Kahikans could hear.

"What do you mean, *artificial* sumati?" Maikee was indignant. "Who do you think you are, coming here and cutting into my profits?"

"Who do you think *you* are, addicting an innocent stranger?" the judge demanded. "We'll have to leave this place sooner or later. Where are we supposed to get sumati *then*?"

"Trade for it," shrugged Nehinei. "The whole universe can come here and trade for it."

"Terrific," Aleria told him, her tone dripping with

sarcasm. "A whole universe full of sumati addicts. I'll put this entire planet on outlaw status before I'll let that happen. No one will be allowed to land here—or to leave!"

"Now, now, Aleria—everyone doesn't become addicted. Look at Jemall."

Aleria did, and saw the bailiff looking very uncomfortable. Was it because of his unaccustomed frog shape—or something else? She remembered then something he had said about the artificial sumati—"You aren't going to like it." *Why?* she wondered. *Side effects, perhaps?* She'd have to ask him, but the thought of turning on that transponder again was more than she could bear. She still had a pounding headache from all those underwater conversations.

Besides, the Kahikans were becoming a bit hostile and needed to be placated.

"Jemall is one of very few Acetans to leave Aceta," she explained to them. "His immunity to sumati is nice for him, but most space travelers are of Earth stock like me. My race seems to have a wanderlust that others do not show. And creatures of Earth—if Rosmer and I are any example—are *very* susceptible to sumati dependency."

Nehinei, at least, was beginning to understand. "There are many of your race?" he asked.

"You've seen the stars in the lahnee at night?" Aleria countered.

He nodded.

"For every star you can see, there is a populated planet somewhere, a planet with far more humanoids than Kahiko's seas support."

Nehinei nodded again. "You are right. We have not enough sumati for so many." He glanced at the Acetan bailiff, who was leaning against Rosmer's tank inspecting the webbing his transmutation had placed between his long, four-jointed fingers. "How does he do it—make artificial sumati?"

Aleria shrugged. "The same way he does everything. Show him, Jemall. Flex your magic fingers, Froggy."

Jemall winced at the appellation, but he glanced about for something to transmute. There was one small coprolite on the beach, left over from the pile they'd amassed earlier for him to use. The bailiff picked it up and placed it on the prince's open palm.

"Watch," he said. Then he began to concentrate on the task at hand. Extending his fingers, flexing them once, twice, three times, he muttered something under his breath.

The coprolite was no longer petrified.

Nehinei looked down in disgust at the object in his hand. "What was it Rosmer said before? Gag me with a prune?"

Aleria glared at the bailiff. "You did that intentionally!"

"Yes," he admitted. "It's the first step. Making synthetic sumati is a two-stage process."

"Well," Aleria told him, and there was no mistaking the command tone in her voice, "get on with it."

Jemall hastily flexed his fingers again, and the object in Nehinei's palm became a mound of fine, pearlescent powder.

"It looks right," ventured the prince. "But will it work?"

"Let's find out," Aleria suggested. Her craving was so great now that she couldn't stop herself from reaching toward the substance in Nehinei's open hand. Indeed, her desire for the drug outweighed even her knowledge of what this sumati had been, only moments ago.

"Bah, humbug," snorted Maikee. "I'm going back to my suma beds, back to the real thing." He dived into the water and disappeared.

But Aleria and Nehinei ignored him. The judge reached

out, as though in a trance, and took a minute portion of the substance from Nehinei's open palm. Nehinei took a like amount. The two of them stared into each other's eyes as each mirrored the action of the other, a hand placing the tiny portion on a tongue.

Their eyes never left each other, Aleria's golden brown locked on the Kahikan's pale blue-green, the blue-green of the Kahikan waters from which he had sprung.

The Kahikan held out his hand to Jemall, who extended his own beneath it. Nehinei dumped the entire mound of synthetic sumati into Jemall's waiting palm.

The bailiff glanced at the judge and the Kahikan, then shrugged and muttered, "Why not?" He poured the entire handful of sumati into his mouth, swallowed, then dusted off his hand.

For just a moment, nothing happened. Then the three of them became a tangle of arms and legs, mouths and tongues, fingers and feelings, silvery, tawny, and that odd Kahikan bluish-greenish mauve, inventing permutations and combinations never before known to man, frog, or sea creature, there on the shining sands of Rix.

Drifting semiconscious in the tank beside them, Rosmer was one with them. Tied to him through the bond of the Ring, so were Carswell, Selmar, and Sebrook—and so, though not quite as firmly, were Levis and Medina as well. Even as Rosmer writhed and gyrated in his tank, so did the three Orono in the space station. Levis and Medina, at the first inkling that another wave of orgiastic sensations was about to hit them, had placed all their monitors on automatic and bolted for the section of the station where the dolphins had taken up residence. Now the two humans stood, mouths agape, before the whirling trio in the tank.

"What's going on?" Medina, cupping her hands around her mouth, screamed with all her mental and vocal energy. The Orono broadcast a picture back to her and to Levis: Aleria, Nehinei, and Jemall knotted in a never-ending tangle on the pale sands of Rix, and the dolphin, helpless in the tank beside them, separate from them and yet one with them, even as the Ring was separate and yet one with him.

"They've got to stop this. Tell him they've got to stop this," Medina commanded.

*Fashoor*, Carswell narrowcast. *But he's sending too powerfully. We can't fight him.*

"If he can reach us, we can reach him."

*Maybe, when this is over.*

"Now!" Medina was clutching Levis's arm. Her shrill command, broadcast both orally and telepathically and augmented by the technician, seemed to break the hold of the broadcast from Kahiko on the dolphin Ring.

"Stop it—now!" she cried again, and the dolphins managed to do just that, to cease their helpless sympathetic whirling and regain control of their own bodies.

*M–Medina.* Selmar was panting. So were the others. Medina had never seen a dolphin pant before. It meant a lot of churned-up water in the tank as the Orono repeatedly surfaced for more air. *Any suggestions on how we get through to them?* he finally managed to ask her.

"Augment with all our might," Medina replied after a moment. "Show them the effect of these broadcasts on us. I have a feeling they don't know."

*But we can reach them?*

"Why not? They're reaching us."

Sebrook was skeptical. *They seem to have some extra power. I sense extra voices in their augmentation. Perhaps the Kahikans—*

"If the Kahikans can help them broadcast this far, they can help them receive, too," Levis suggested.

*That doesn't always follow*, Carswell protested.

But Medina and Levis were already stripping off their jumpsuits and sprinting for the tank. Once in the water, Medina locked one arm around Levis and reached out with the other for the nearest dolphin, who happened to be Carswell. Levis reached out his free arm to Sebrook. Selmar swam into position so they could touch him with their feet.

"I'll create the images," Medina told them. "You latch on to them and *send*!"

The others flashed an acquiescence.

Medina thought a moment, then constructed the mental image she wanted to send. "Now," she ordered, and they all latched on to the image and sent it with all their might.

Helpless in the throes of sumati, Aleria *was* all her nerve ends, feeling every grain of sand beneath her, every smooth scale that brushed her body. And she was both of her companions, even Jemall who—having ingested more sumati than any other creature had ever dared—had suddenly awakened to the telepathic sensations of his companions. He *was* Aleria and Nehinei, they *were* the big Acetan.

Aleria felt her long, four-jointed fingers moving—no, those were Jemall's—toward her own tawny thighs, parting them, reaching between them toward that most sensitive spot on her body. Even as she felt those fingers on her, she also felt that long alien tongue on the sensitive edge of her now-sealed gills, felt the tickle as her hair brushed Nehinei's chest, felt the eerie sensation as his sinuous organ emerged from his body, felt it reach out for her, felt it touch her in ways she'd never been touched before.

She *was* the dolphin in his tank, writhing spasmodically in combined pleasure and pain. She was other dolphins in another tank, another man, another woman, watching her, feeling her sensations even as she felt them, begging her to stop, ordering her to stop.

*Oh, my god*, she thought, *we're broadcasting all the way back to Earth!*

*How wonderful!* exclaimed Nehinei.

*How embarrassing*, corrected Aleria.

*How exhausting*, complained the other woman. *You'll have to stop.*

*We can't!* Aleria replied, and showed them. Her body was not her own. It belonged to the sumati, to the others to whom the sumati had joined her.

*You must*, came the reply from the Ring.

*You must!* echoed Rosmer from the tank beside her, from inside her mind.

But Aleria was reaching out blindly, all physical sensation and mental conjoining, and she could not stop, would not stop, didn't want to—

*Stop!*

The order, sharp and shrill, came from the Ring and the two humans augmenting it.

*Stop!* Rosmer's voice joined in. *Sumati is murder. Sumati is genocide!*

*Silly*, Aleria chided him. *Sumati is love.*

*Sumati is death*, Rosmer told her, told them all. *Sumati is the reason we came here, the death of a race.*

*How can that be?* asked Nehinei, his hands and tongue and organ still engaged, even as his mind left the orgy to enter the conversation.

Aleria flashed him an image of their mission to Kahiko. *Someone—some race—is being annihilated.*

*It's the Suma*, Rosmer said mournfully. *They are intelligent, though immobile. Their telepathic voices are weak, almost as mute as the Acetan's. They had to merge them all to send us their appeal for help.*

*But how are they being annihilated?* Nehinei protested. *We don't allow them to be killed.*

*Nevertheless, they are dying off—and you do not allow them to reproduce.*

*Ridiculous*, Nehinei countered. *We protect every creature that even looks as though it might grow into a Sum.*

*No*, replied Rosmer, *you do not. You devour their young—all of their young. Their young are the sumati!*

# Chapter XIV

"I told you that you wouldn't like what I'd found out," Jemall told Aleria. They were lying on the sand, inches apart, yet afraid to touch each other for fear they would set that demanding sexual empathy in motion once more. Nehinei lay a few feet beyond, curled up in a ball, the picture of utter misery.

"Well, now we know why Rosmer kept muttering about shame and guilt," the judge replied. "I share his feelings. He and I *need* sumati. Without it we'll surely go mad, perhaps even die. But to use it is to kill the children of another intelligent race. How awful!" Then she sighed with relief. "Thank heaven you were able to manufacture synthetic sumati."

Jemall shrugged. "I wasn't sure it would work, you know."

"You weren't?"

"Sumati is composed of living creatures. I cannot create life—not even from the bacteria in unpetrified coprolites. I had the chemical elements right, but I wasn't sure if it was the chemical or the living essence of the sumati that produced its effects."

Aleria smiled. "It seems to have been the chemicals. My need for the stuff was certainly assuaged. But you took so much—"

"How do you know?"

"I saw it in your mind, while you were linked to us," the judge told him. "Are you feeling any cravings?"

Jemall shook his head. "Not at all. It was an interesting experience, but I feel no need to repeat it."

Aleria, who was beginning to feel those faint stirrings of need once again, doubted his words. Jemall had practically overdosed on synthetic sumati, yet he claimed to be immune. How could he be? "Now even a tingle of a craving?" she asked him.

"Not a one."

"Well, *I* still need it. And Rosmer must be even worse off. We'd better give him some of this synthetic stuff before he gets the deetees."

Jemall looked blank. "What are those?"

"An old Earth term for a reaction one gets during detoxification. I don't know how it originated. But I've seen the condition. It's awful." Aleria shuddered. Detoxification was what lay in store for her—and for Rosmer—unless they wanted to be dependent on Jemall's synthetic sumati forever.

Slowly, reluctantly, Aleria pulled herself to her feet. Her legs were still shaky from her physical exertions. Had all that really happened only a few minutes ago?

She walked over to the tank, feeling awkward on land after all that time in the sea. She clambered up the ladder and leaned over the waters through which the dolphin slowly swam.

"Rossy," she called, "Jemall's made some synthetic sumati—a sort of methadone. No clams were killed to make it. If you need—"

*But I don't!*

"What?"

*I don't have any craving for the stuff, so I have no intention of touching it ever again.*

"No craving? None at all?"

*None.*

"But—but how?"

*I don't know,* said the dolphin, *but I do know one thing. Now that I'm safe here in the tank, safe from fenoki, safe from Rautgut, safe from addiction, and since I've managed to solve the problem we were sent here to solve—*

"Correction," Aleria told him. "You've identified it; you haven't solved it."

*In any case, I'm not leaving this tank,* he announced. *Not until I'm back in my home waters with my Ring. Fashoor—totally.*

Aleria shook her head. This was the old Rosmer, all right. But what could have cured the powerful need he had exhibited such a short time ago? Could it have been communication with his Ring? But that would have meant it was just a psychological rather than a physical addiction, and—

*Communication with his Ring!* They had actually been in two-way communication with the Ring—and the Ring was lightweeks away, even through the warp!

"Rossy, do you realize—" she began, but he interrupted her, accurately reading her thoughts.

*I'm still in contact with them. I didn't want to break the link, lest I lose it—but it's growing stronger by the minute!*

"Sort of like exercising a muscle? The more you use it, the stronger it gets?"

*Yes, exactly,* the dolphin affirmed.

"Rossy, this is a real breakthrough in interstellar communications. Imagine never needing to wait for a drone again!"

*The problem is, it only connects beings who've already formed a deep connection, like my Ring. And I can tell you fashoor that you're never going to get Orono into space again. No way.*

Aleria, who was starting to feel that need for sumati building inside her again, was beginning to wonder why she'd ever gone into space herself.

"Rossy, can I talk to them, too?"

*Sure. Just augment.*

"It's easier in water. I'm coming in." She dived into the tank, swam over to the dolphin, and opened her mind to the Ring.

Aleria found that carrying on a conversation with a Ring of dolphins was a disconcerting experience. They tended to express themselves in mental images that were complete thoughts. Sometimes these flashes took more time to process than the Ring allowed her before hitting her with yet another image. When they did use language, they tended to insert those strange phrases that they claimed were native to their oceans—things like "Grody to the max," or "Kiss my tuna." Finally Aleria resorted to asking them to let her speak with the woman whose voice she had heard overriding the confusion of the multiple link. The judge wanted facts expressed in human terms as only a human could express them. Besides, she realized, she was hungry for the opportunity to converse with someone of her own species.

Medina's mental voice separated itself from the babble of the link, and Aleria forced herself to lead off with what was potentially the most damaging inquiry: how far-reaching had those broadcasts been and how identifiable?

Medina's reply was somewhat reassuring: *The effect was felt all over the monitoring station, but I don't think anyone outside the Ring—and Levis and me, who were plugged into it—knew what was causing that effect or who was involved.*

Aleria sighed deeply. *Well, that's a relief. But tell me, how are we going to explain this kind of communication without blowing our cover and letting on how we discovered it?*

*Actually, Levis and I were thinking of keeping it under wraps until we can figure out how it works*, Medina told her. *Right now the only reason we can converse like this is because we're both connected to this Ring. No other Ring has ever been able to do anything like this before.*

*Have the members of any Ring ever been separated by the interstellar void before?* the judge countered.

*No, of course not. But the Ring couldn't converse with Rosmer until just now. We tried earlier and were unsuccessful.*

Aleria's mind flashed back to the earlier image that had authorized her to rule on Kahiko's application to join the Confederation. Medina verified that the Ring had sent it. *But*, she added, *interstellar telepathic conversations like this one have never been possible—until now.*

*Do you think we were really able to form this link on our own?* Aleria asked. *Or did we need Nehinei? Kahikans are pretty powerful telepaths, you know.*

*He could have caused the breakthrough*, Medina agreed. *But there's only one way to test it. We'll have to break off communications and then try to reestablish them—with Kahikans and without them.*

*I'm game,* Aleria said. *Rossy?*

*No!* The homesick dolphin flatly refused to break the mental link with his Ring.

*Come on, Rossy. It's for science,* the judge cajoled. *If we can't reestablish it alone, I'm sure that Nehinei will help us.*

*What if we need more sumati to make the connection? I'm not touching that stuff again.*

*I'll bet we won't even need Nehinei.*

*But we're taking a chance on losing contact with the Ring—my Ring!* Rosmer managed to make this sound as though it would mark the end of the universe. He remained stubbornly silent for a long while. At last he agreed to break the link—but only if the Ring would promise to remain in the most receptive stance possible, with Levis and Medina augmenting to enhance its powers. *And if we don't get through to you within a standard half-hour,* he insisted, *you try getting through to us!*

The Ring agreed, and the link was severed, though by which of its participants it was hard to say.

The sudden mental silence felt strange to Aleria, after having her mind populated by the thoughts of others—and so many others—for so long. She could truly empathize with the dolphin's distress at his separation from the Ring; she was feeling a little lonely and abandoned herself now that the connection had been severed.

"Let's give it a couple of minutes before we try to reestablish contact," she suggested reluctantly. "Just to make sure it's a totally new contact."

Rosmer conceded the wisdom of waiting and passed the time doing sad little dives and leaps. Aleria leaned back and floated on the surface of the water, enjoying the sensation as her long red hair billowed loosely about her.

The waters of the tank felt somehow different from the waters of Kahiko, more comfortable, almost soothing. Aleria felt more buoyant, too, as though a great weight had been lifted from her. And in truth, she *was* more buoyant, for the water in the tank was more saline, and the saltier the sea, she remembered, the better it supported you.

Only then did she realize just what weight had been lifted from her—her craving for sumati was gone!

For just a moment, she reveled in the sensation of owning her body again, free and clear of the lien the sumati had put on it. Then she turned back to the dolphin to verify that his need, too, had ceased to exist.

"Rosmer? Did you say you didn't want, didn't need sumati anymore?"

*Fashoor.*

"Why not?"

The dolphin pondered for a moment or two. *I don't know. Does it matter?*

"Yes—because I don't think *I* need it anymore!"

*Way totally tubular!* Rosmer exclaimed.

"Huh?"

*An old Pacific Dolphin expression. I'm really pleased for both of us. What do you think cured us?*

Aleria thought about it. "Maybe the link?"

*That would mean it was merely a psychological dependency. It certainly felt a lot worse than that.*

"I know what you mean. But what else could have done it?"

They both fell silent for a moment. Then Aleria splashed to an upright position. "Rosmer," she shrilled, "it's the *salt*! We've found the antidote!"

Rosmer considered and then concluded that the salt had probably brought about their cure. *However*, he added. *I am not about to readdict myself to test your theory.*

Aleria was inclined to share that sentiment. "Maybe we can handle this without empirical testing," she suggested. She opened the transponder channel to Houston, who stood on the field at the opposite end of the island. *Houston, do me a favor.*

*Your wish is my command.*

*It ought to be—I'm your commander*, she reminded him. *Listen, do you have the chemical analysis for sumati?*

*Yes.*

*See if sumati dependency in an Earth mammal could be affected by exposure to salt.*

She could almost hear his circuits humming. But after a moment or two she could sense that the dolphin was beginning to grow anxious—and she realized that the business at hand was the reestablishment of the link. *Houston*, she interrupted, *will this take very long?*

*Shouldn't. I'm almost—done!*

*Well?*

*You're right. Sumati addiction is based on an electrolyte imbalance. In Earth mammals, reestablishing the proper electrolyte balance cures the addiction—and apparently epidermal exposure to a sufficiently saline solution affords that.*

*Fantastic. I wonder if it would work for the addicted Kahikans, too?*

*No way to tell. I don't have enough data on their body composition and functions.*

*Well, I can't wait for you to work that out. Rosmer and I have to try to reestablish the link.*

*Link?*

Houston didn't know! Aleria had forgotten that he couldn't know her thoughts unless the transponder was activated. When Jemall's overindulgence in synthetic sumati had allowed him to break the telepathic barrier, Aleria had just assumed that there were no more barriers to telepathy, that there were just slow learners. But Houston was a *machine*; all of his functions were mechanically or electronically induced. Telepathic communication without a transponder was not one of them.

*Ask Jemall. He'll explain*, she told the ship. Severing the connection, she turned her attention back to the dolphin.

"Houston has just confirmed that exposure to enough salt is the cure for sumati dependency. One problem solved. Now let's see if we can link up with your Ring again."

She swam over and wrapped her arms around the dolphin, trying to establish a physical as well as a mental bond. She let down all the barriers of her mind, opened it to him, and began the most powerful augmentation she had ever experienced.

She could feel Rosmer reaching out to the Ring, reaching, reaching for the link across the vastness of space.

Nothing happened.

"Damn," Aleria muttered. "We can't do it ourselves."

*Let's get Nehinei*, Rosmer suggested. *We've got to reach them again!*

Aleria swam over to the tank wall and called to the Kahikan. "We need your help," she explained. "We can't seem to reestablish the connection by ourselves."

"Anything for a friend," Nehinei replied and bounded over the wall into the water.

But he winced as his supple body plunged into the highly saline solution in the tank. "This water hurts," he protested.

"That's impossible," Aleria replied.

"Nevertheless, it does. Let's reestablish the link now, so I can get out of here."

"Right."

The three of them, joined together, seemed to have a telepathic power that was greater than the sum of its parts. Aleria could feel their minds reaching out across the vastness of the interstellar void, homing in on the waiting dolphin Ring on that monitoring station near Sol 3.

The linkage was explosive and implosive, both at once, something like a tsunami rushing to meet a giant suction pump. Then they were suddenly—the three of them—one with each other, one with the Ring, and one with Medina and Levis, too. The force of the joining took their breath away.

*Whew*, Aleria broadcast when she managed to get her lungs and gills working once more. (Which was it? Who was she? All of them? none of them?) *I don't think we'll have to try quite that hard the next time.*

*I'll second that.* The mental voice belonged to Levis.

*We needed Nehinei*, Aleria pointed out, *but the rest of us may have been unnecessary—or necessary for directional purposes only.*

She turned to thank the Kahikan and suddenly was able to pinpoint the raw, gnawing pain that she was sensing through the link. Nehinei was in agony. The salt water seeping beneath his scales felt like a million tiny darts, like in army of fire ants.

The Kahikan was beginning to turn colors, a rainbow of colors, not the colors that he turned when in the throes of sumati, but angry, dark colors, stress colors.

*We'll have to carry on without him*, Aleria ordered. *Nehinei, get out of here!*

But the Kahikan prince seemed to be paralyzed with pain; he did not move. What if he were dying? She grabbed his shoulder and shook him, but he failed to respond. It suddenly occurred to Aleria just how hostile the Kahikan waters could have been for her without this alien prince at her side. She remembered, too, his brother's distrust of things—and beings—that disturbed the status quo. She needed Nehinei.

More than that, she liked him. She didn't want anything to happen to him. She certainly didn't want him to die.

*I guess you'll have to hold the link without me, too,* Aleria told the others, and she broke away physically to drag the Kahikan to the edge of the tank and boost him over the wall.

"Jemall," she called to the bailiff, "Nehinei's been poisoned by the salt in the tank. Get him into his own waters, quickly!"

The big silver bailiff bounded over on his muscular legs and scooped up the limp Kahikan prince. He covered the width of the beach in a single bound and deposited Nehinei—still changing colors—into the gentle surf.

It took several anxious moments before Nehinei's color stabilized. At last he seemed to relax as he lay there in Jemall's arms; he even stopped his shuddering. When he opened his eyes, Jemall turned to wave at Aleria. "He's all right," the bailiff called to her.

"I can see that," she called back. "I'm rejoining the link." The bailiff nodded, and Aleria turned her attention back to Rosmer and the rest of the Ring.

The link had held, even without her. Apparently, they needed Nehinei to establish it but not to maintain it. But could Aleria have maintained it alone, as Rosmer had done while she was aiding the Kahikan? *I can see that this is going to take a lot of experimentation*, she noted.

*We're going to apply for a grant*, Medina told her. *This could be a major breakthrough in interstellar communications*

*What if it requires a Kahikan in every port—and one on every ship?* Aleria wanted to know.

*We'll cross that bridge when we come to it*, the other woman replied. *Rosmer has filled us in on the developments on Kahiko. What are you going to do about the annihilation of the Suma?*

*It's a real problem*, Aleria said. *Some of the Kahikans are addicted to sumati, but apparently the cure that works for us could kill them! I'd like to admit Kahiko to the Confederation of Planets, because we'll need their talents if our guesses about these links prove out. And if we admit Kahiko, we can police the planet to protect the Suma.*

Then she pondered for a moment. *I'll just have to sell them on Jemall's artificial sumati. I'm sure it can be manufactured as well as transmuted. Maybe they can set up their own factory to make it. If not—*

*If not*, Medina finished for her, *that planet's going to start out with a lousy balance of trade, and it's only going to get worse.*

*Unless*, Aleria said slowly, *unless—*

She cut the thought short. *I'm going to convene a hearing*, she told the others. *Tell Judge Ashippun that I think I have the problem licked. I'll call in when I've got the results. I do have carte blanche, don't I?*

*You do*, Levis and Medina assured her. *The drone confirming it should be arriving any day.*

*Life's little ironies*, Aleria chuckled. *But I think every-*

*thing's beginning to fall into place here*. She severed her connection to the Ring and bounded over the wall of the tank, then down the beach to where Jemall and Nehinei waited at the water's edge.

# Chapter XV

Nehinei reacted edgily to the plan Aleria outlined for the Kahikans. "I don't have the right to ask anyone to give up sumati," he protested, "least of all those who are addicted to it. If that's the condition for our admission to the Confederation, perhaps we shouldn't join."

"Wasn't the synthetic sumati just as effective?" Aleria challenged.

Nehinei nodded dismally. "Of course, but—"

"There's more to it than just the addiction, isn't there?"

The Kahikan prince was silent for a moment. At last he looked up, his discomfort apparent in his sea-colored eyes. "All of my power—such that I have—is based on the crown's ownership of the Suma beds. If no one is dependent on the crown's favor for sumati any longer, I will wield no power."

"That's no problem," Jemall shrugged. The Acetans were a practical people, given to expeditious solutions. He had one now. "We'll just give the crown the franchise for synthetic sumati."

"You're saying we'd have to import it, then? We couldn't make it here, ourselves?"

"You don't have the raw materials," Jemall told him. "To get them you'd have to process rocks, shells, and huge quantities of seaweed. For that, you would need a manufacturing plant capable of breaking down those substances. Just where would you put that plant?"

"Anywhere you want it." The Kahikan gestured magnanimously.

"It would have to be on dry land."

Nehinei glanced about at the limited acreage of the only island on Kahiko. The landing field took up half of Rix; the other half, containing the customs office and the Port of Kahiko, was hardly bigger than Rosmer's tank, which now stood on the sloping beach, nearly covering it. "I guess we couldn't put it here," he conceded. Then he brightened. "You could transmute us another island!"

"Sorry." Jemall smiled apologetically. "I don't think that's included in my job description."

Aleria smirked. "Neither are a lot of the other things you do, but you do them anyway. Why not make them an island?"

"Nope. Sorry," said the Acetan, and it was apparent that he really was sorry. "Another island would totally disrupt the flow of the waters. It could change the entire character of the ocean bottom. I can't take the responsibility for that."

"We wouldn't hold you responsible," Nehinei promised, but Jemall was adamant.

Aleria tried a different tack. "We could order an environmental-impact study," she suggested.

"Don't need one," Jemall demurred. "Houston has

calculated the effect already. We know it shouldn't be done."

"So we'll have to import?" Nehinei sank to his haunches, the picture of dejection, and absently ran his webbed fingers through the shiny sands.

Aleria tried to encourage him. "It won't be that bad. I'm sure we can keep the price down. And, as Jemall suggests, the crown can keep the franchise. After all, there's no sense in disrupting a planetary economic system that works."

"What about the sumati-barss?" Nehinei wanted to know. "They won't want to to go back to being ordinary citizens again. They like their isolated, rough, tough way of life. They like the power that harvesting sumati gives them."

There was no getting around it: sumati-barss could never live in the cities. Like Maikee, they would return to their Suma beds. And even if *they* didn't mine them, the Suma were still open to attack from Rautgut and any other predators who might be partial to sumati. That gave Aleria an idea, and she said as much.

"Well, don't keep us in suspense," the Kahikan demanded.

"I'll tell everyone when the time it right. First, let's set up that hearing on Kahiko's admission to the Confederation."

"Hearing?" Nehinei asked. "Who said anything about a hearing?"

"Well, I *am* a judge."

"But, but—"

"And that *was* a hearing room you showed me, wasn't it?"

Nehinei nodded morosely. "We haven't had a hearing

there for aeons—not since my people developed conveying to the art that it now is."

"Well, I'm going to hold a hearing. That's my job," Aleria informed him. "You can call in representatives of whatever factions exist on this planet—sumati-barss, addicts, what have you—and they can all have their say. Then I'll make my decision."

'It sounds to me as if you've already made it," Jemall told her, sotto voce.

"No comments from the peanut gallery," she hissed back at him.

Jemall was nonplussed. "What the heck is a peanut gallery?"

Aleria thought about it. "I don't know," she replied. "That's just an old human expression. It probably goes back as far as Rosmer's 'fashoor.' The origins of both are undoubtedly lost in the mists of the past."

The Kahikan was squatting on the strand, looking very confused. "What happens at a hearing?"

"I'll hear all sides of the issue. Then I'll render my decision and you can spread the word. Assemble your very best conveyors and anyone else who wants to be heard."

The Kahikan looked skeptical, but his colors, which had been darkening with stress, began to return to normal. He took a deep breath. "I'll set it up. Meet me at the entrance to the Great Cavern."

"When?"

Nehinei looked up at the sky. The pale Kahikan sun was approaching its zenith. "When the sun over Rix is halfway to darkness."

Aleria nodded. "That's about three hours. See you then."

The Kahikan dived into the waters, leaving the judge and her silver bailiff alone on the sand.

\* \* \*

Aleria had forgotten how vast the domed cavern was. Without Nehinei's humming to distract her, she could see that its arched gray walls were very distant from its sunlit center, and she noticed for the first time how many concentric rings of columns there were between the well and the walls.

*You understand our protocol?* Nehinei broadcast to her.

*I was going to ask you about that*, the judge replied. *I assume that the testimony will be taken here in the center of the room?*

*Yes. You and those with statements to make will occupy the center of the chamber, beneath the beam of light from the lahnee. The Council—*

*Who?*

*My royal relatives.*

*Oh.*

*They'll swim in the first concentric ring. Beyond that, the guards will swim. They'll be just ceremonial, I hope.*

Aleria hoped so, too, and told him so. Nehinei went on with his description.

*And beyond that, the conveyor corps will swim. Then any spectators who show up.*

But Aleria was less concerned about the spectators than about the press. *How reliable are the conveyors?* she asked him pointedly.

*They are our swiftest swimmers, our strongest sounders, our most powerful telepaths. They are chosen for their broad and accurate memories—*

*That isn't what I asked.*

*—and for their integrity.*

Aleria was relieved to hear it, for she realized that these conveyors would not only spread the word of today's hearing across the Kahikan seas but would also pass the story on to their children, to be retold for generations to come, since an underwater culture did not develop paper and ink—or even cuneiform. She was relieved at the thought that today's historic events would be recorded accurately as possible, given the lack of technology on Kahiko.

The participants and spectators were beginning to arrive. Aleria, watching them, started as a school of small red fish descended through the well, their mental voices a babble of nonsense. Nehinei directed them toward the far wall.

*What are they, and what are they doing here?* Aleria wanted to know.

*They are heerings.*

*Herrings? Red herrings?* She couldn't believe her ears.

*Heerings*, Nehinei corrected her, *are semi-intelligent, like the kolenya, and can be trained. You can use them to mask private conversations that you don't want conveyed. They can raise their mental voices on command in order to do so.*

Aleria was hard put to stifle a giggle. She had never seen *real* red herrings before. And if their babble was used to distract, that was exactly what they were, even if they were called *heerings*—appropriate enough in a *hearing* room!

The heerings were followed by a variety of Kahikans, some accompanied by their children, some with kolenya in tow. Nehinei busied himself directing them to their appropriate places. And just as he had predicted, as soon as the various groups reached their proper distances from the midpoint, they began to swim in slow concentric circles around the judge. This had a rather dizzying effect; it was rather like standing in the center of a carousel, and Aleria began to feel just a bit light-headed.

She forced herself to look away from the circling fish and Kahikans, concentrating on the dusting of golden sand that was washing back and forth over the porous stone floor, pushed by the currents generated by the swimming throng. Conducting a hearing in the middle of this chaos would be impossible! Then she was forced to hide her amusement as she recalled some of Judge Ashippun's advice when she first took the bench: "One of a judge's duties is to keep things moving in the courtroom." *That* certainly wouldn't be a problem here in the Great Cavern of Kahiko!

As the Kahikans continued to file into the room, Aleria noticed several of Jemall's transmuted mermaids among the throng. Each seemed to be surrounded by an abundant male entourage. Apparently, there was something about fish-tailed women that males of any species seemed to find particularly attractive, and always had. The mermaids seemed quite happy in their new form, and Aleria suspected they would continue to refuse to be transmuted back to their original shape. Jemall's influence on Kahikan lore and legend would certainly be a lasting one, the judge reflected. She knew that she ought to log in the origins of the mermaids for the sake of those who would do the Confederation's formal planet study, but she was more than a little reluctant to elaborate on the reasons for the women's transmutation—though she realized that sumati was such an integral part of Kahikan society that she could blame virtually anything on its influence.

Still, mermaids were the stuff Earth legends were made of, from Homer to Hans Christian Andersen. She remembered an old sea chanty she had been taught as a child, about a lighthouse-keeper who had "slept with a mermaid one fine night." That union had ostensibly produced a porpoise; she wondered what Rosmer would say to that!

*Not much*, intoned the dolphin's mental voice in her mind. She'd forgotten he was augmenting her, so that her telepathic force would be powerful enough to conduct this hearing without the assistance of the Kahikan prince. She hadn't wanted it to look as if she was taking sides—or as if Nehinei was. And her own telepathic capabilities, even though they had developed considerably since she'd come to Kahiko, were still not powerful enough on their own.

*Were you eavesdropping?* she asked the dolphin.

*Couldn't help it. You weren't screening.*

*Oops—thanks for reminding me!* There was always so much to remember when you conversed telepathically. Aleria was beginning to look forward with surprising eagerness to her return to normal spoken conversation.

Reluctance, rather than eagerness, however, characterized Nehinei's behavior when it was time to commence the trial. She knew he was not looking forward to his people's reaction when he told them they would have to give up sumati. But the Great Cavern was full, and the hearing could not be put off any longer.

*Nehinei*—she began, but he held up his hand. Moments later, a troop of sumati-barss, led by Maikee, arrived through the entrance well.

There was no mistaking the open hostility of the sumati-barss. Their life-style was being threatened, and they didn't like it. The sumati-barss were an unfriendly bunch to begin with, and, if anything, the group with Maikee was more taciturn, more aloof, more threatening than he had ever seemed to be. For that matter, Maikee himself now seemed openly hostile. Aleria hurriedly opened the transponder channel to Jemall and summoned him to her side for protection. The telepathic abilities he'd developed through his use of synthetic sumati were limited at best, and they were rapidly diminishing.

*Boy, will I be glad when I can leave my privacy switch on, and you can only get into my head in emergencies,* the bailiff remarked, as he made his way through the throng to join the judge.

*I know,* Aleria agreed. *Using the transponder this much has given me a headache that may never go away.*

*Well, I hope you don't think I like being privy to your thoughts,* the ship piped in. His addition to the link was necessary in order to maintain it, and Aleria remarked sourly that being connected to machines was one of the main reasons she disliked the transponder. Houston was less than appreciative of her comments, but the judge ignored him.

Now that her bailiff was at her side, Aleria wanted this trial—which, she realized, could prove very trying indeed—over with as soon as possible. She summoned Nehinei. *Let's get this show on the road.*

Nehinei looked at her, puzzled. *Show? Road?*

*An old Earth expression,* she explained. *I mean, let's get started. Jemall usually calls my courts to order, but his telepathic voice will never be heard over the din of this crowd. You'll have to do it—and introduce me.*

*I know.* Nehinei's reluctance was almost tangible. But he posted a conveyor in the center of the well above them and called the hearing to order.

Nehinei was not without his powers of persuasion. Before he introduced her, before he even mentioned her purpose on Kahiko, the prince first flashed images to the crowd of previous traders who had visited the planet, and of the things that trade could bring them—glass, underwater lights, fire, blasters.

He worked the crowd like an expert. By the time he'd shown them, through mental pictures, what a blaster could do to fenoki and Rautgut, his audience was with him all the way, and highly in favor of joining the Confederation.

*However*, he cautioned them, *there are obstacles to our being accepted for membership.* He explained, then, the true nature of sumati and the fact that the Suma were intelligent creatures.

Aleria could feel the horror of the crowd. She listened carefully as Nehinei summed up his position: *So you see, even if they were not intelligent, we would defeat our own purpose by driving them to extinction. But since they are an intelligent life form, we are morally obligated to stop devouring their young.*

But before the impact of this statement had time to soak in, Maikee stepped forward and began to address the crowd. He threw out a mental image of need for sumati—mild need, stronger need, and then the most severe kind of craving. He broadcast the agony of withdrawal and the pleasure that the use of sumati brought.

His argument was more than convincing. The crowd was with *him* now, and hostile to the strangers who had come to take their sumati from them. Aleria could feel their angry murmuring from the outer rings where they swam.

Nehinei turned to her with a helpless gesture. *What do I do now?*

*Introduce me*, she ordered.

But it took him a long, anxious moment to get the attention of even a few of them. Their minds had been turned against the prince, and they were no longer interested in what he might have to say. Maikee commanded their loyalty now. He and the other sumati-barss also seemed to be blocking—or drowning out—Nehinei's attempts to broadcast.

*We've got to get through to them*, Aleria transponded to her bailiff. She glanced at the circling swimmers, and they seemed suddenly menacing, more menacing—because of their sheer numbers and the enclosed space through which they swam—than even the Rautgut had been. *Jemall*, she urged, *you're the bailiff. Call this court to order. Do something!*

The Acetan reached for his blaster.

*Not that!* Aleria hissed. *That's for defensive use only.*

He shrugged. *It could come to that, but I wasn't going to shoot anyone. I needed something to transmute.*

He removed the spare power pack from his holster, set it on the cavern floor at his feet, and flexed his fingers at it. Nothing happened.

*A fine time for you to mess up a transmutation.* The judge glanced nervously at the angry throng. Maikee's goading seemed to be stirring them to greater hostility every moment. *Hurry!* she pressed the bailiff, knowing his psionic transmutation powers could not be hurried, but hoping that her words would somehow speed them.

He flexed his fingers once again, and again nothing happened. He looked up at her helplessly. *I think something in the water might be messing me up.*

*You didn't have any trouble before. Try again. Hurry!*

Jemall rolled his shoulders, as though to relax them. Then he extended those long, four-jointed fingers one more time. The power pack disappeared, and in its place lay a small depth charge.

Setting that off would be a drastic measure, all right.

Aleria turned to the Kahikan prince. *Nehinei, have you been able to get through?*

*No.* His mental transmission had the tone of a frustrated wail.

*Well, cover your hearing organs,* she advised, and, putting her hands over her own ears, she nodded to the bailiff.

The depth charge was a small one, but, set off within the confines of the Great Cavern, it reverberated, echoed, seemed to tear through Aleria even though she'd been prepared for it. Its roar bounced back and forth within the dome and seemed to last forever. But it served its purpose: the swimming crowd came to a wavering halt.

When at last the shock waves had abated, and utter silence reigned, Aleria turned to Nehinei.

*Now, introduce me,* she ordered. He did.

The stunned assemblage listened in respectful silence, first to Nehinei's introduction, then to the flame-haired judge who now commanded the central position, bathed in the shaft of light from the well.

Aleria thought it would be difficult to maintain an authoritative tone when speaking in images rather than in words, but the depth charge had established her authority. Now, as she extolled the virtues of synthetic sumati, she could feel her audience growing receptive to her arguments. She called on Nehinei to provide further testimony, and he conveyed a description of the potent effects of the sexual methadone Jemall had developed.

But Maikee and the other sumati-barss sneered at the idea of a synthetic substitute for the real thing. The crowd wavered, unable to decide between the two sides, and Aleria had no choice but to launch into the next phase of her plan.

*You're sure that what I'm saying is being conveyed, exactly the way I'm saying it?* she asked Nehinei.

*All over the planet*, he assured her.

*Good*, she muttered grimly. And, dredging the depths of her mind for the memory of every commercial she had ever seen, she began an advertising campaign like no other that had ever existed. She hit the Kahikans with a barrage of images, all borrowed: "New," "improved," "taste that leaves the others cold," "richer, fuller." "Progress is our most important product," she told them. "Good to the very last drop." "More powerful than a locomotive"—was that an ad? "More doctors recommend . . . ." "Tell a friend." "Extinction is forever." And, finally, "Try it—you'll like it."

The spectators had resumed their circling. They were now more relaxed, and she could sense them beginning to consider her arguments. But the sumati-barss would not be moved. Aleria knew she could not allow them to resume their arguments, for the shock effect of a depth charge would only work once. If she lost the crowd again, a second explosion would only make them more hostile, perhaps even aggressive.

There was nothing for it but to drown out any protests with a barrage of mental images of her own. She quickly launched into an outline of her plan for the new Kahikan economy.

Kahiko would have to trade for synthetic sumati and for the other trade goods Nehinei had shown them, she conceded. She explained to the Kahikans, through a series of images, how they could use their brilliant red netting as an export, and she explained that the balance of trade would be skewed if they didn't have other trade goods as well. Then she pulled her trump card.

*Kahikans have a talent needed by the other members of the Confederation,* she told them. Their telepathy, she went on to explain, could be used to connect distant planets and ships traveling through the vast emptiness of the interstellar void. Kahikans could name their price for such services and then collect whatever the traffic would bear.

*The only Confederation race that even approaches the telepathic powers of the Kahikans does not travel well,* she continued, flashing an image of the difficulties of transporting a dolphin through weightless space. *Their telepathic abilities are not nearly as great as yours, and since you Kahikans are amphibious, you can live in spaceships as you do on Rix. Those of you who choose to travel as conveyors can change the balance of trade in favor of Kahiko. This will be a very rich planet.*

*Why leave Kahiko?* Maikee snorted, but Aleria had anticipated his challenge. She began to broadcast a mental portrait of something she knew well and loved even better— the lure of the vast reaches of the galaxy, the mystery of the space between the stars. Working with images was suddenly easier than working with words, for she could now show the Kahikans what was in her soul—her love for deep-space travel, the adventure of it, the secrets it revealed.

With the help of Nehinei and Rosmer, she broadcast a vision of that vast diamond-studded blackness, the glory of a living planet seen from beyond its atmosphere. She sketched the stars as pinpoints of cold fire in the empty distance, and sang the serenade that the solar winds played out there in the void where, always, new stars were beckoning, calling, urging you on.

There was a kind of rapture to the solitude of travel through the emptiness between constellations, and you felt an eerie oneness with all that had ever existed, would ever exist, when you cut through a warp. Red stars, white stars, yellow stars, planets that were barren and planets that were lush with greenery, planets that boiled with sulfur or ammonia, planets that were blanketed with benign nitrogen-oxygen atmospheres, carbon planets, silicon planets, living planets, dead ones.

She showed them a sunset on Mondovi, which many travelers considered the most beautiful planet in the universe, and the six moons of Tagenet, all shining at once. She showed them swirling desert sands, golden beaches, tropical rain forests where thick curtains of greenery blotted out all but narrow shafts of light. Tall forests, barren moonscapes, the fragile crystal life forms of Manieren, and the graceful batwings found on Largissent. *And you can have it all*, she finished, *all of it. But only if you protect the Suma.*

She could sense that many of her listeners had been moved by her visions of the universe, but Maikee and the other sumati-barss refused to allow themselves to hear her. They countered with images of the Kahikan deeps, memories of the ecstasies of sumati, the oneness of Kahikans here on their own world. And they protested the loss of their independence, of the lonely, rugged existence they loved.

But Aleria had yet another card up her sleeve. She overruled them by broadcasting an image of the Suma as helpless victims of the Rautgut even if the Kahikans ceased to prey on them.

*They must be protected*, she stressed. *It will take a fierce and independent breed of Kahikan to live so far from civilization, to be the lone bastion against the evil Rautgut. Such persons would be highly respected, I'm sure. They might even become, in time, the heroes of legends.*

Aleria could sense that her appeal had touched the sumati-barss, who rather liked the idea of being solitary rangers—all except Maikee, who would not be moved. Well, she would concentrate on the others.

*Remember*, she reminded them, *you don't have to give up the throes of sumati. We have synthetic sumati that is just as good, if not better!*

*I don't like it*, Maikee said bluntly.

*Maikee doesn't like anything*, Nehinei told Aleria. *That's why he lives out there with the Suma. You'll never get through to him.*

But Aleria felt she had to try. She flashed Maikee a private picture of their experience together when he'd introduced her to sumati, and her own experience later, using Jemall's construct. But she sensed the Kahikan pushing the images from his mind. *Won't you just try it?* she pleaded. *Just once? Just think how much more weight your opinion will carry if you reject it after giving it a trial!*

That argument was the kind that appealed to the stubborn sumati-barss; he capitulated and consented to try the synthetic sumati. *But I know it won't work*, he emphasized, *and I intend to say so.*

*Just try it*, Aleria urged. *Then you can say whatever you like.*

Maikee stepped forward and opened his mouth. Aleria could tell by his awkwardness that he was far more accustomed to being the sumati-giver than the recipient. Following Kahikan custom, she placed a minute quantity of synthetic sumati on his tongue, then waited.

The sumati-barss stood immobile, the only unmoving creature in the swirling cavern. Aleria could feel the scorn of the crowd: The synthetic sumati wasn't working. Then Maikee began to convey—first surprise, then delight, then rapture!

A mental whisper went up from the crowd: *He likes it. Maikee likes it!* The other sumati-barss surged forward to try it for themselves.

Then the circling crowd began to move in. Aleria swam up toward the well, but the Kahikans followed her, the circles in which they swam contracting as they moved toward her. Fearing that they would crush her, Aleria threw caution to the winds; with a broad gesture, she scattered the entire contents of the container of snythetic sumati through the waters that swirled and roiled around her.

The currents generated by the swimming Kahikans carried the sumati throughout the vast domed cavern. Soon everyone in the cavern—adults and children, heerings and kolenya—all were exposed to the substance. Aleria, too, as the waters flowed through her gills, began to feel the now familiar effect of sumati on her psyche.

*Rosmer, screen!* she ordered, then broke her connection with him, in one last, desperate effort to keep from broadcasting this experience to the rest of the universe. And then she could not, would not fight the enticing sensations any longer. Inside herself, outside herself, one with all the others in the cavern, she moved toward Jemall, Nehinei, Maikee, felt them move toward her.

This was the reverberating cavern in which Nehinei had first seduced her with his humming. Now he was humming again, as were Maikee, the other sumati-barss, and all the other Kahikans. The tone was hypnotic, enticing, demanding. It cut through her very soul, into her being, vibrating along every nerve, turning her bones to jelly. At the base of her skull, at the back of her neck, up and down her spine, the humming set up sympathetic vibrations, and she was humming, humming, too. The walls themselves seemed to be vibrating as well as reflecting the sound. The great coral columns undulated with it. And the concentric circles of Kahikans closed in on them, moved outward, came closer once more, then once again moved farther away.

Kahikan dreams invaded her mind, Kahikan sensations invaded her body—Kahikan thoughts, kolenya images, cool darting little fish babble from the heerings. Up and down her body, her nerves carried the sensations of her own grapplings and desires and the desires of a hundred other creatures, alien and familiar, sensations in organs that she recognized, sensations in organs she had never known existed, and through it all, those vibrations, that humming, setting her very soul on edge, with every nerve ending reaching for more, always more.

And she was reaching out for Nehinei, for Jemall, for Maikee, for the kolenya, for shining fish tails, red—the heering?—and green—the mermaids?—reaching with her hands, her mind, her soul, reaching with organs she did not possess but knew the feel of; she was one with the others, and they were one with her, humming, humming, warm, cool, undulating, swimming, floating, lost in the world of sumati, lost in the sweeping sensation, a rapture of the deep that no earthly diver had ever known.

Through it all, her own visions—burning stars in the blackness of space, a sunset on Mondovi, the eerie oneness of the warp—were fed back to her by those to whom she'd broadcast them only a moment ago, yet back before time and the planet had begun. Suddenly she possessed alien memories, too—oki stands and Suma beds, near misses with Rautgut, hatching (was that heerings?) in the cool mud of the ocean bottom. And then the conveyor corps opened its mind, conveying all of Kahikan history so that she and they were one with the past, the present, the future, united with one another, never and forever all lost in the now.

It was sensory overload in the best and worst sense. Soaring, floating, exploding in the light, sinking into cool darkness, Aleria was one with the whole of Kahiko, plunging, plummeting, sleekly cutting through the water, being born, giving birth, dying, living, even flying above the waters in the graceful leap of a flying fish. It was too much, it was too little, she wanted more, she couldn't possibly take any more, she wanted it to stop, she hoped, begged, prayed it would go on forever. Inside herself and outside herself, the world existed in light and darkness at the same time, then faded into nothingness that was both relief and deprivation, cool emptiness where the sudden silence that was the absence of humming became a fierce roaring in her ears.

# Chapter XVI

She drifted back to consciousness on the surface of the water, uncertain of how she had got out of the cave, not even sure whether she was, in fact, still alive. Then a vague hunger, a craving like an itch in the back of her soul, convinced her that she was—yes, alive, and again addicted to sumati.

"Well, we get to test the salt theory empirically," she muttered, and she turned over and began to swim toward the distant pinpoint on the watery horizon that must be Rix. "Let's just hope salt will work a second time." She didn't want to think about the consquences if it didn't.

It might have been easier to swim beneath the waves, given her altered form, but Aleria felt she needed the sheer physical exertion to clear her head, and she chose to cut along the surface of the water in a powerful crawl. The webbed feet and strong leg muscles Jemall had given her propelled her more easily than her own legs ever had before her transmutation, and the webbing between her fingers caught the water, thrust it behind her, expediently, efficiently. She had become, through Jemall's agency, a creature of the water, and she covered the distance to the landing field in record time.

One question burned in her mind with even more intensity than that of whether salt would end sumati addiction a second time, and she voiced it immediately. "Did you screen?" she demanded of the dolphin as she came up the beach beside his tank.

*Yes, but it wasn't easy. I had to sever the link again, and the sensations you were conveying—so many of you— were overpowering. I think the only thing that saved my sanity was being in a separate body of water.*

"Well, I'm about to join you in that separate body of water. Move over."

The dolphin was wary. *You're not still in the throes of sumati, are you?*

"No. But I need to take the cure again."

*That means that the synthetic stuff is as addictive as the real thing. I was afraid of that.*

"Yep." Aleria clambered into the tank. "It's like scratching an old itch. It doesn't take long to get hooked a second time." She plunged into the water and sat on the bottom for a time, cross-legged, brooding, not saying a thing.

*Is it working?* Rosmer asked, after a while.

Aleria shot to the surface and shook the water from her eyes. "I think so. Yeah, I guess it is."

*So the cure will work more than once. That's good to know. Still, I wouldn't want to risk it a second time.*

"I wouldn't either if my addiction had been as severe as yours. Orono must be really sensitive to sumati."

*Actually, I'd had several more exposures to it—in small amounts—before our time in the tortoise*, Rosmer confessed.

"You did? You never said so."

*I'm good at screening.*

"Where'd you get it?" Aleria asked him. "And when?"

*Back before you and Jemall took to the waters—remember?*

"Why, Rosmer, you old roué, I thought you were far more conservative than that."

*It's a façade I like to adopt. I'm the soul of discretion.*

"Let's hope so. You're going to have to keep a lot of secrets for both of us." Aleria glanced distractedly around the island. "Have you seen Jemall?"

*I think he's in the ship.*

The judge nodded and sprang over the tank wall, then took a leisurely stroll over to where Houston stood, gleaming in the morning sun.

"Hi, Houston. Is Jemall around?" she asked casually.

"About time you got back," was the ship's sour response. "He's inside fooling around with my data banks. He's been at it for the past three days."

*Three days!* Aleria was horrified. She'd figured she had lost one night, but not three! Clambering up the ladder into the main cabin, she announced to the ship and the bailiff, "Boys, we've got a problem."

"Only one?" asked Jemall.

"One bad one. We've got to teach the Kahikans to convey only when—and what—it is essential for them to convey. They've got to learn to stop conveying during scenes like—"

Jemall nodded. "I know. I've been working on a handbook."

"Handbook?" the judge asked. "For whom?"

"For the Confederation Conveyor Corps. How do you like the title I gave them?"

"It has a certain ring to it," she replied. "What kind of handbook?"

"It's a guide to subjects that are taboo in the various cultures of the inhabited planets. Bekeho did a comprehensive study, you know."

"I remember—and you can trust her data; she doesn't fudge," Aleria mused. "Do you think we can get the concept of taboos across to the Kahikans?"

"If we can't, then we *are* in trouble." Jemall flashed her a quick grin, then returned to his work with unusual dedication. Aleria suddenly remembered that sex for pleasure was frowned upon on his home planet, and she wondered if he had an ulterior motive for embarking on this project. Protecting the sensibilities of his fellow Acetans meant protecting himself as well, for if word of his adventures ever got back to them, he'd be in even worse trouble back home than he was now. Leaving Aceta with knowledge of psionic transmutation was a capital offense. Only Aleria's quick talking had got him off the hook for that—and it was only a temporary reprieve. If he ever fell into Acetan hands—well, it just made sense not to antagonize his fellow Acetans any more than he had already. No sense in letting them know how he passed his time.

Aleria sat down at the other computer console. "Houston," she told the ship, "while Jemall is working on that handbook, let's get the conditions for Kahiko's admission codified."

"You sure are lucky I can do two things at once," the ship asserted archly.

"Listen, buddy, you've been sitting on your ass for weeks, doing nothing but connecting our transponder links."

"You think I enjoy that?"

"I think you derive a certain vicarious pleasure from it," Aleria informed him. "You're the worst kind of prude—a closet voyeur."

The board at which she was sitting suddenly went dead. So, apparently, had Jemall's, for the bailiff complained, "Now look what you've done. You've insulted him, and he's switched off. I just hope he stored all that data first."

"You've made him do this often enough," Aleria reminded Jemall. He and the ship were usually at odds. "You know what to do. Just hit the override."

The judge and the bailiff reached for their override buttons in unison, and their consoles hummed back to life. "The truth hurts, doesn't it?" Aleria asked the ship. "You overreacted."

Her console started to dim again, but she hit the override button, at the same time announcing in very clear tones, "There seems to be something wrong with the computer on this vessel. We may have to replace it."

"You wouldn't dare." Houston's voice had a wariness that hadn't been there before.

"Try me," Aleria said grimly. She could have sworn she heard the ship gulp. "Now, about that codification." The proper format appeared on the screen before her. "Thank you, Houston," she told him sweetly, and she could have sworn she heard him sigh.

It took several hours to get the admission statement worded the way she wanted it and to iron out all the ambiguities. By then, Jemall had finished his handbook. Aleria logged the order in, then asked Houston to send a drone containing the full document back to Confederation Central. At last she stood, brushing her hands against each other in a symbolic gesture. "Nothing left but promulgation, Jem. Let's go find Nehinei."

That did not prove difficult. The Kahikan was sitting on the beach in front of Rosmer's tank when the judge and the bailiff emerged from the ship. The first words out of his mouth were, "They'll accept the synthetic sumati."

"I'd guessed that." Aleria sat down beside him on the sand. "I've drafted the conditions for Kahiko's admission to the Confederation."

Nehinei looked at her expectantly. "What are they?"

Aleria began to read. " 'The Planet known as Kahiko, formally designated as Nihal Four, is hereby admitted to the Confederation of Planets on and under the following conditions: first, that the recognized intelligent species on this planet number three, namely the Kahikans, the Suma, and the Rautgut. These species are granted self-determination and may apply to the Confederation for protection from enslavement and annhiliation.' "

"The Rautgut have rights?" gasped Nehinei. "You didn't say anything about that before."

Aleria nodded. "They have rights, but so do you. If they attack you, you have the right to fight back, but the Confederation frowns on preemptive strikes."

Nehinei sighed deeply. "Well, they'll probably stay in their own territory, anyway. At least, I hope so. What else?"

Aleria picked up where she'd left off. " 'Second, all existing governments of the planet are hereby recognized.' "

"There is only one," Nehinei reminded her.

"I know—but, just in case, I've recognized whatever form of government the Rautgut may have."

"Oh."

" 'Third, all interplanetary trade shall be licensed by the authorized government. The government shall have the right to restrict, regulate and tax all off-planet trade.' "

The prince smiled. "Sounds good."

"I thought you'd like that," Aleria told him. "There's more, though. 'Fourth, Kahikans have agreed to preserve and protect the status of the Suma in the name of the Confederation. The Kahikan government shall appoint Rangers to defend the various Suma beds on the planet Kahiko. Payment for this duty shall be made by the Confederation in coin of the Kahikan realm, a substance called sumati, which shall be manufactured off-planet and delivered to Kahiko at regular intervals.' "

"That should make Maikee happy," Jemall remarked, and Nehinei nodded in agreement.

"That will give you a basic supply of sumati," Aleria noted. "*Synthetic* sumati, that is. You can trade for more of it, if you want to, or for other goods."

She returned to the proclamation. " 'Fifth, the use of any but synthetic sumati, anywhere within jurisdiction of the Confederation, is hereby prohibited, and the export of natural sumati from Kahiko is likewise prohibited, and any violation of this prohibition shall be punishable as a Class B felony.' "

"Whew—heavy!" Jemall commented. He explained to Nehinei that the punishment for a Class B felony was life imprisonment on a penal asteroid. Nehinei thought that punishment quite appropriate, now that they knew that sumati consisted of sentient creatures.

" 'Sixth, all synthetic sumati used or sold anywhere within the jurisdiction of the Confederation shall carry on it the visible statement that the use of sumati has been determined to be highly addictive and maybe hazardous to the health of the user. And seventh, we hereby establish the Confederation Conveyor Corps. No one may serve as a conveyor unless he or she agrees to abide by the rules and regulations of the corps, as appended hereto.' "

"What kind of rules?" Nehinei wanted to know.

Aleria turned to the dolphin in the tank beside them. "Rosmer, do you have any suggestions for explaining this to Neninei and his people?"

*I could link with him and show him, using images,* the dolphin offered, *but he has to promise to reconnect me to my Ring afterward. I had to break the link during that hearing.*

"It's a deal," agreed the Kahikan, "as long as I don't have to get back into your tank again."

But after Rosmer had explained the concept of taboos to him, Nehinei was almost too embarrassed to reopen the link to the Ring. Only Aleria's reminder that he had promised to do so, in a contract that she had the authority to enforce, persuaded him to act. And once he had made the connection, the Kahikan left hastily, returning to the waters to explain to his people the conditions of their admission to the Confederation.

Rosmer was delighted to be reunited with his Ring and would have been content to spend his time dreamily communing with them, but Aleria insisted on being put through to Levis and Medina. Her first order of business was to determine whether Rosmer had, indeed, been able to screen out any transmission of the hearing. She was greatly relieved when Levis and Medina denied any knowledge of what had transpired there.

*But there* was *a kind of sexual itchiness,* Medina reflected. *About three days ago, I think.*

*Let's not mince words*, Levis teased. *The two of us got horny as hell. But it seemed to be limited to us, so we figured it was our problem, not one caused by waves of conveying from Kahiko.*

*Wrong*, said Aleria. *It was a wave from Kahiko, all right, but Rosmer screened it, so I guess it only reached sensitives—and maybe only the two of you because you've been linked to us.*

*What are you going to do when Rosmer leaves Kahiko?* Medina asked, alarmed. *How will you screen then?*

Aleria explained the Conveyors' Handbook, and her rules for the admission of Kahiko to the Confederation.

*Sounds as if you covered all the bases*, Levis noted.

The judge smiled. *I hope so. Listen, a drone is on its way, but would you mind giving Judge Ashippun a preview? I want him to know how it went.*

*No problem*, Medina told her. *I'll call him.*

*Great. We're going to tie up a few loose ends here and then head for home. I look forward to meeting both of you in person.* Then the judge and the technicians abandoned the link to the members of the Ring.

There were fewer loose ends than Aleria had thought. Conveying was a shortcut to making others understand something. Nehinei was able to make the concept of taboos comprehensible to all of the Kahikans. The rules, too, were conveyed and understood.

Aleria called the sumati-barss together to swear them in as Suma Rangers. Jemall did some fancy flexing of his fingers and created a badge, blaster, and holster for each of them, and they strutted about the beach proudly in their new finery.

Maikee was put in charge of them. "You understand," Aleria cautioned him, "that, although the other rangers are answerable to you, *you* are answerable to the Confederation for their actions. I expect you all to abide by the rules."

Maikee appeared to be taking his responsibility very seriously. Aleria administered the oath, first to him, then to the others, then gave them all their first month's allotment of synthetic sumati in advance. Jemall had been busy transmuting it all day from stray shells and coprolites. As Aleria noted, there was no sense in putting temptation in the way of a hungry man. Jemall had also made enough sumati to fill the national coffers, so that the addicts' cravings could be assuaged. No one would need natural sumati now.

"What about all the sumati we've already collected?" Maikee asked.

Aleria remembered his cache, which he kept in shells hanging near the roof of his tortoise-shell home. She pondered a moment, then replied thoughtfully, "I've got an idea that might work. Come on."

The two of them swam off swiftly through the cool Kahikan waters. Now that the route was familiar to her, it seemed to Aleria that it took far less time to pass the oki stands and the coral city, and to come at last to the ancient tortoise shell that marked Maikee's turf.

They swam into one of the larger openings in the front of the shell, then up to the cache just below the dome. Gathering as much sumati as she could carry without spilling it, Aleria headed for the Suma bed, with Maikee, similarly burdened, close behind her.

*Have you ever tried to communicate with a Sum?* the judge narrowcast at the sumati-barss.

*I never realized one could*, he told her quite honestly.
*Well, let's try now.*

They set down the shells containing the sumati, pressed their bodies against each other for as much contact as possible, and then lay full length across the largest Sum in the bed. *I'm going to try to convey an image*, Aleria told Maikee. *Help me put it through.*

The image she created was one of a sumati-barss defending a Suma bed from Rautgut. Aleria drew it clearly and carefully, and sent it with all her might. She felt Maikee conveying just as hard.

Then they stopped and waited there, in close contact with each other and the Sum.

There it was—a faint feeling of gratitude—or was it? Perhaps she was only sensing what she wanted to sense. She could not be sure, and the Kahikan wasn't certain either.

*Let's try again*, she told him. This time she chose an image of Kahikans forswearing the use of sumati.

Again they conveyed with all their might, and again they waited. This time, they were sure they felt it—gratitude. The Sum was thanking them.

*Now*, Aleria told Maikee, *one more time*. And this time the image was of a sumati-barss, in badge and netting, replacing previously harvested sumati into the muscle of a Sum. *Concentrate*, she told herself.

Maikee, who was at first surprised by the image, took it up enthusiastically, conveying it to the Sum with all his might.

This time Aleria knew that they had gotten through. This time the answer came back so clearly that there was no mistaking it. It was a wave of gratitude so strong that it brought tears to the judge's eyes. And as Aleria and Maikee pulled away from the giant Sum, they saw a sight never seen before in the waters of Kahiko: all of the shells in the Suma bed began to open slowly, ever so slowly, to receive their stolen offspring once again.

# Chapter XVII

*No. Absolutely not.* The dolphin was adamant.

They were preparing to leave Kahiko, and Jemall had made a very logical suggestion: Why not turn Rosmer into a land mammal for the duration of the trip, so that they wouldn't have the burden of transporting his tank and maintaining the artificial gravity?

"Why not, Rossy?" Aleria cajoled. "It doesn't hurt. I've been running around with gills all this time, and it hasn't bothered me. And those mermaids seem to love their new shapes."

*I like my old one.*

"But it would only be for two weeks. Just till we get back to the monitoring station."

*No, I won't take the chance; he might mess up in changing me back. No way.*

Aleria had to concede that Jemall didn't always get his spells right. That was what came of leaving school before his training was finished. But he'd done exceptionally well here on Kahiko. She said as much to the dolphin.

*All the more reason not to press our luck*, Rosmer replied.

Aleria sighed. "I guess that means we'd better get the tank aboard. Rossy, you'll have to wait in the water while we do it."

*As long as it doesn't take you too long.*

"You know," Jemall reminded the judge, "I enlarged the tank when we set it up here on the beach. I'll have to reduce it again."

Aleria thought a minute. "Maybe not," she mused.

"Aleria," Jemall complained, "on the way out, we couldn't get near each other because that tank took up too much of Houston's cabin. It's a two-week trip."

"I know."

"But if we put the tank in the way it is, we won't be able to play with ourselves, let alone with each other."

"Interestingly put," Aleria replied, "and just what I was thinking."

"So?"

"So why don't we keep these amphibious shapes until we get back to the monitoring station? Then we can ride back in the tank instead of outside it. That will solve the playtime problem."

"You mean—?" the bailiff began.

"Exactly," the judge told him. "If you can't beat 'em, join 'em."

Jemall's groan was so loud that several Kahikans poked their heads up from the waters to see if he was okay. Aleria waved them off with the information that no one had ever died of a bad pun. But Jemall was less certain.

He was also uncertain of whether Rosmer would welcome their company, now that he was no longer in the throes of sumati, but Aleria knew better. She told the bailiff about Rosmer's earlier adventures.

"So that's where he kept disappearing," Jemall smiled sagely.

They were interrupted by Houston announcing the arrival of a drone messenger.

"Don't tell me—" Aleria began. She put the message through the transcriber, read it, and chuckled. "We are authorized to investigate Kahiko for possible admission to the Confederation and to ascertain who or what might have sent that distress signal. I have full discretion in making my decisions."

"Isn't it nice to know you had the authority you exercised?" Jemall asked.

"It *is* nice to have it in writing, even though telepathy is so much faster."

"True. But it can be unnerving," the bailiff recalled. "Which reminds me, I'm not playing any games with Rosmer unless he disconnects that link. I don't want our adventures broadcast to kingdom come."

Aleria smiled slyly. "I don't really care if a kingdom comes," she winked at him, "just so *you* do!"

Then she ran for the ship and disappeared through the hatch before he could transmute a coprolite back into its original form. He meant to pelt her with it, but he hit the ship instead, and Houston didn't speak to him all the way home.

*Watch for*

KINGDOM COME

the third novel in THESE LAWLESS WORLDS

*coming in October!*